# CHASING
# SHADOWS

*To Rivo Lockhart
My friend for
all time.
Marie Duncan Caldwell*

*Alan Tucker*

# CHASING SHADOWS

*a novella by*

# Marion Driscoll

*with* Alan Tucker

MAD Design, Inc.
Billings, Montana

Copyright ©2012 by Marion Driscoll and Alan Tucker

First Edition

ISBN 978-0-9826864-9-2  (paperback)

*Dedicated to
the Wounded of All Wars
and the memory of
the Yankee Division*

# Margot

## *July 4, 1958*

**"T**he world would come to a grinding halt if it weren't for paperwork," Dr. Margot Braun grumbled to herself, slowly pecking at the keys of the Smith-Corona on her desk. Shortly thereafter, the thin sheet of carbon paper wadded up hopelessly in the rollers and she threw her hands up in disgust.

Pat Boone crooned softly from the radio sitting next to a stack of reference books on the credenza where most folks kept their typewriter. Margot's desk chair was a hand-me-down from one of the other doctors in the facility and refused to adjust any lower than its highest point, causing her toes to barely touch the floor, and her knees to bang painfully into the credenza.

Margot sat back in the chair, which responded with a loud creak, and folded her arms across her chest. Looking down, she noticed a small, dark smudge on her white smock, probably from the recalcitrant carbon paper. Closing her eyes, she allowed Pat's smooth voice an attempt to relieve her jangled nerves.

The afternoon had been relatively quiet. Most of the staff was off for the holiday, and would be for the long weekend as well. Being new, Margot had drawn the short straw to be the doctor on premises. Being a woman, Margot knew she'd be drawing that same straw for the foreseeable future. She didn't really mind though; the hospital was peaceful without the hustle and bustle of its normal staff complement. She had finished her last set of rounds efficiently, then returned to her small office to catch up on paperwork.

Margot sighed and turned her attention back to the typewriter. Pat had done his job well. She carefully removed the papers and inspected the copy. Thankfully, the crinkled carbon hadn't left any errant marks large enough to render the second sheet unusable. She tossed the ruined carbon in the wastebasket beside her desk and removed a fresh sheet from the drawer on her right.

"That was Pat Boone with 'I'll be home.' Hope you're having a great Fourth of July," the radio announcer said in a voice indicating he was not. "It's a scorcher out there. Ninety-two on the thermometer. We'll have more music right after a few words from our sponsors."

After turning the volume down on the radio, Margot delicately lined up the two forms she'd been working on with the new carbon in between. Her windowless office was never adequately lit, but it did at least provide protection from the summer heat. Bookshelves lined the walls to either side, covering the whitewashed brick that dominated the building.

The speaker in the intercom box above her door crackled. "Dr. Braun to the front desk, please. Dr. Braun, to the front desk."

Margot chuckled at the formality in Edith's voice. The facility may have been short staffed because of the holiday, but that would never stop the elderly woman from following protocol regarding intercom announcements.

Curious what prompted the call and welcome for the interruption, Margot rolled back and hopped down from her obstinate chair, once again considering the benefits of spending her own money on some office furniture that didn't make her feel like a misbehaving ten-year-old.

She crossed the short distance to the door in two strides and entered the stark hallway. The ever-present hint of ammonia tickled her nose. Margot sniffed to avert a sneeze. Turning left, she marched down the corridor to the reception area of the facility.

The Colorado State Hospital, in the city of Pueblo, had been built in the late 1800s. It housed and cared for a large number of the state's mentally ill. Some were criminally insane, and held in another building on the grounds, but the majority were simply those who could not care for themselves and didn't have families either in a position, or willing, to accept the responsibility.

Margot had received her doctorate in psychiatry nearly ten years before, but the task of landing a permanent position anywhere had proved difficult. She had signed on for a few postgraduate research projects until funding had dried up, then she'd bounced around the Midwest, taking what work she could find. When she heard about the position in Pueblo, she jumped at the opportunity, even though the pay was far less than a doctor was likely to expect elsewhere. It was enough to make ends meet and Margot had a strong desire for stability in her life.

The reception area was only slightly less utilitarian than the rest of the building. A plain, tan leather couch, flanked by two equally drab chairs, sat to the left of the glass entryway. In front of the couch, a long dark coffee table held a small assortment of old magazines and an electric fan worked overtime to push the sun's heat back toward the front door. The only piece of decor that didn't serve a specific function was a large painting of a mountain scene, by an unknown artist, hanging on the wall opposite the couch.

Directly across from the glass doors, Edith Merriweather primly performed her duties as gatekeeper to the facility from a glass-front cubicle with a small counter and pass-through for paperwork.

Standing at the counter, writing on a clipboard, was a tall young man dressed in a pressed white shirt with dark pants. His blonde hair was slicked back and he wore a look of concentration on his smooth face, no doubt trying to decipher the form Edith had produced for him to fill out.

Next to him, in a wheelchair, sat a tired-looking elderly man with unfocused eyes. His greying hair was unkempt and he had a day or two's growth of beard on his gaunt face, the left side of which was slack and droopy.

The young man looked up from the clipboard and smiled as Margot entered the room. Before he could speak, Edith stood up and said, "Ah, Dr. Braun. This is Mr. Milichuk, down from St. Luke's in Denver.

"Pleased to meet you ma'am," the young man said, extending a hand in Margot's direction.

She took it and returned his firm shake. "Likewise, Mr. Milichuk. What can we do for you?"

He nodded toward the man in the wheelchair. "Got a John Doe here for you. Someone brought him in last week — found him along the bank of Turkey Creek west of town. Anyway, docs barely saved his life — said he had a major stroke — but he's got amnesia. Can't even remember his name. Well, long story short, we haven't had anyone come lookin' for him and we needed to clear out some beds — always some burn and heart attack victims on the Fourth, you know — so, the docs said to ship him to State."

"I see," Margot said. She knelt in front of the chair and looked into the man's vacant eyes. "He's stable?"

"Yes, ma'am. Docs gave him some painkillers for the ride down here. No tellin' if or when he'll have another stroke, but they said they've done all they can. And with no kin to claim him …"

Margot knew the private hospitals were never big on indigent care. No money in it. "All right. We'll take him from here. Have a happy Fourth of July, Mr. Milichuk."

"Thank you, ma'am," he said with a broad smile of clear relief. Evidently the doctors at St. Luke's hadn't been positive the patient would be accepted. Margot hoped the man didn't have some other condition they'd been reluctant to reveal. "You as well. His file's right here, what there is of it," he said, pulling a folder from a pocket at the back of the chair.

She accepted it and nodded her thanks.

"All right then," the young Mr. Milichuk said. "I guess I'd better get myself on the road."

"Drive safely," Margot said as he waved on his way out the front door. She turned her attention once again to her newest patient. "Very well, Mr. Doe, let's see about finding you a room."

It was nearly suppertime before Edith had been satisfied with the forms for checking in John Doe and the two of them had him resting comfortably in a bed. Margot then saw to her duty of portioning out medications for the patients who needed them with meals. She followed one of the kitchen staff around, distributing food and medicine and checking in on those who were bed ridden or otherwise restricted to their rooms.

The clock in her office read almost half past eight when Margot returned to find her neglected paperwork sitting patiently next to her typewriter. She sighed, moving around the desk to sit in her awkward chair. It was then she noticed a new addition to the clutter in her workspace: a file placed at the top of her in-basket. She picked it up and saw the neatly typed "John Doe" on the tab. She'd nearly forgotten about their newest patient with all the work surrounding the evening meal.

She sighed and reached for the thin silver chain around her neck that held her wedding ring, running her finger along the smooth, finely wrought links. The staff at the hospital weren't allowed to wear rings, for a number of reasons, so she kept hers on a necklace rather than leave it at home. Closer to her heart, as she thought of it.

Margot had met Harold Braun four years earlier, shortly after she'd found a job in St. Louis, moving from Norman, Oklahoma. Her car broke down upon her arrival and a kindly, dark-haired mechanic took pity on her, fixing it for free. He'd also offered to take her to dinner. Normally she would have refused, but she felt guilty for her inability to pay for the work, and besides, he was a handsome sort.

She'd never thought her work would allow room for a steady relationship, let alone marriage, but Hal — only his mother called him Harold — had been more accommodating of her career than she could have ever dreamed. "A good mechanic can find work anywhere," he had told her once.

Margot picked up the telephone receiver and dialed home.

"Hello?" Hal's baritone voice sounded far away over the line.

"Hi, it's me. Still at work."

"Mmhmm. Comin' home soon?"

She glanced at John Doe's folder. "I've got one more thing to check on. Might take me a bit. Did you find something for dinner?"

"I just boiled an old boot," Hal said with a chuckle. His famous ineptitude in the kitchen was a running joke between them. "Kinda stringy, but not bad."

"Save me the tongue then."

"Are you kiddin'? I ate that first!"

Margot laughed. "Scamp!"

"Some guys at work said there'd be fireworks at the Fairgrounds, probably around nine," Hal said, hope in his voice.

She glanced at the clock again and sighed. "You better go without me. I'll meet you there if I can make it."

"All right. Be careful drivin' home," he said. She could hear his disappointment, but felt his calm acceptance as well.

"I love you."

"Love you too."

Reluctantly, she hung up the receiver, then opened the thin folder in front of her. The ambulance driver, Mr. Milichuk, had been right about there not being much in the file. No medical history, of course, since they couldn't identify the patient, just a report on the work they had done to save his life. The doctor who had performed the exam was clearly surprised Mr. Doe had survived. It spoke of a strong heart. Results of blood work done showed a high level of alcohol — evidently Mr. Doe had been drunk when he'd suffered his stroke. Because of the long time frame involved from discovery to care, the doctors were unsure whether their treatments had been effective, or Mr. Doe had simply been lucky and the clot that caused his stroke had broken apart or dissolved on its own. They noted the resultant partial paralysis of the patient's left side, as well as the sedatives and other subsequent treatments they'd administered.

Then, having no next of kin to contact and no one asking about anyone by his description, they had released him after eight days.

Margot closed the file and sat back. She wondered what the man had been doing at Turkey Creek and how he'd gotten there. She knew of migrants and homeless people who lived outdoors in the summer months in this part of the country, but that answer just didn't seem to fit with her first impression of Mr. Doe.

She got up and searched her shelves for a volume or two on memory loss, then hung her white overcoat on the rack next to the door. Her stomach grumbled. The few bites of stew she'd had during the dinner hour were long gone. Margot took a handful of saltine crackers out of a desk drawer, then locked up and headed out, waving goodbye to the night staff as she left.

On the drive home, Margot saw a flash of color in the distance, then heard a concussive double boom a second or two later. She hoped Hal had gone out to see the display. A small smile crept across her lips. Maybe they could create some fireworks of their own once she got home.

# Margot

## *July 5, 1958*

**M**argot opened the door to John Doe's room after quickly noting, from the call sheet attached to the wall, he'd been conscious and had eaten his breakfast earlier in the morning.

The tiny room had only space enough for a single bed and a small table and chair. She found Mr. Doe sitting up in the bed with his pillow cushioning his back from the curved metal of the headboard. He looked up at her entrance, alert on the right side of his sallow face, but slack and unresponsive on the left.

"Good morning, I'm Dr. Braun," Margot said as she closed the door and pulled the chair closer to the bed. "Did you enjoy your breakfast?"

Mr. Doe nodded. "It wasss filling," he said with a strong slur, the paralyzed portion of his face making speaking difficult. "Not much for tassste."

Margot chuckled. "That's true. The cooks around here are not known for their overindulgence with spices. How are you feeling?"

"Okaaay." After a pause, he added, "Tired."

"Understandable after what you've been through." She pulled a notebook and pen from her coat pocket. "Have you been able to remember anything? Your name? Where you live?"

His brow furrowed in concentration, then he shook his head. "No. I ammm wondahinnng where I am. Thisss room is different."

"Yes. You've been moved from St. Luke's in Denver to the Colorado State Hospital in Pueblo." She did her best to gauge his reaction to her words. Those who knew their facility cared for the mentally ill often had feelings of distaste or mistrust. Mr. Doe seemed to take the news in stride, whether from ignorance or acceptance, Margot couldn't tell. She did notice some saliva running from the left corner of his mouth, down his chin. Taking a dry cloth from her other pocket, she reached over and dabbed his face, which colored slightly with embarrassment.

"Sssorry," he slurred.

"No need to be sorry. Some partial paralysis is relatively common in victims of stroke. Can you remember anything about what you were doing before you became ill? You were found along Turkey Creek."

At first, he shook his head, then his right eye widened. "Fisssshthing," he said.

"Fishing?" Margot asked.

He nodded.

"Were you by yourself? How did you get there?"

Again he concentrated, struggling with his wounded brain. "I remembah riding in a truck," he said at last. "I don't know who the drivah wasss. But I think he wasss hauling tires wessst sssomewheah."

Margot quickly scribbled notes. "Can you think of anything he said to you?"

He paused in thought. "Yesss. He sssaid, 'Well, good luck, Chrissstophe,' when I got out of the truck."

"Christophe!" Margot said. "That must be your name. What do you think? Does that sound right?"

He shrugged a shoulder. "I guessss. I can't really sssthay for sssure."

"Well, I'm making a note of it, Christophe, and we'll go with it for now. You really didn't look like a John to me," she said with a smile.

He did his best to smile back, but she could tell his heart wasn't in it.

She leaned closer to him and said, "Christophe, I want to help you. You must have some family out there somewhere who are worried about you, but maybe don't know where to look."

He didn't offer a response, so she continued. "I'd like to try a different technique with you. To see if we can jog some more of your memories loose. If you're willing. It's called hypnosis. Basically, I will help you get to a state of wakeful sleep, for lack of a better description, where I can help you unlock things in your mind that are currently hidden away for one reason or another."

Christophe nodded. "I've heard of that. Bunchhh of mumbo jumbo I thought."

"It doesn't work on everyone," Margot said. "But the results can be quite astonishing. I have to ask that you trust me to give it the best chance of success."

He smiled and she caught a glimpse of what must have been a handsome man in his youth. "You're the doc, Doc."

Margot had spent time with the books she'd taken home while Hal had slept peacefully next to her. Some of her postgraduate work had involved studying the effects of hypnosis, and she'd recently seen some articles chronicling successes with the technique in patients with memory loss. The idea had excited her and she'd hoped her new patient would be amenable to giving it a try. "Let me go fetch some things I need. Would you like anything? Something to drink, perhaps?"

"That sssoundsss good."

"Okay, I'll be right back." Margot left the room and headed for her office, excited to begin. She'd told him the truth when she'd mentioned family who might be searching for him. She just knew in her gut there was someone out there somewhere who cared for him.

In her office, she quickly gathered a handful of books she'd selected earlier and a small gold pendant she'd brought from her jewelry box at home. She then made her way to the kitchens, stopping briefly to inform Edith of her whereabouts and ask not to be disturbed for the next hour or two. Once Margot acquired a cup of fruit juice, she retraced her steps to Christophe's room.

Her armload of possessions made opening the door difficult, but she finally managed and set her things on the table. She reseated herself and helped Christophe take a drink of juice and he smiled his thanks.

"Are you comfortable?" He nodded in response. "Okay," she said, setting the cup aside and taking her pendant from the table. "Please, just relax and focus your vision on this. Think back to the day you went fishing ..."

# Christophe

## *June 27, 1958*

I shivered in the chill air, walking west on the edge of the pavement. Early mornings in the mountains of Colorado were cold, even in the summer. My hips ached, as they often did, and the ever-present knot in my belly announced itself with a stab of pain.

Holding my fishing pole in the crook of one arm, I took a swig of whiskey from the flask in my jacket pocket and told the knot to go sink itself.

I'd gotten lucky and hitched a ride to the edge of town, then, for the next half hour or so, I'd been heading into Turkey Creek Canyon on foot. If I kept my pace, I'd make it to my favorite fishing spot around noon.

I loved to fish. But today fishing was just an excuse to be alone and get stinking drunk.

I heard the rumble of an engine behind me. Out of habit, I stuck my thumb out and, to my surprise, I heard the engine downshift. Looking back for the first time, I saw a flatbed truck, with tall wooden railings, hauling a load of tires. I stopped and waved. The driver waved back and rolled to a stop a few feet ahead of me. Cursing my hips, I jogged up and opened the passenger door.

"Where ya headed?" the driver asked. He wore a dirty ball cap over a head of dark, wiry hair. His face was weathered and friendly.

"Going fishing on the creek, up the road a ways," I said.

"Hop in," he said with a smile. "Don' reckon you'll catch anything if you don' git there 'fore it gits too hot."

I thanked him and hauled myself into the seat. He ground the transmission into gear as I closed the door. After a couple of unsteady lurches, the truck was moving down the road.

"Name's Will," my driver said, holding his hand across the cab toward me.

"Christophe," I replied, giving a firm shake. Will's hand was worn and rough, like my own.

"You fish out here a lot?"

"When I can." I wasn't in the mood to chat, but since Will had been kind enough to pick me up, I did my best to oblige him.

"Where's yer tackle box?"

I patted my breast pocket. "I don't have many lures. I always figure if I bust a line, or it gets too gnarled to untangle, it's time to quit anyway."

Will laughed at that and moved the truck's engine through two more gears and we picked up speed. The old beast was in need of a tune up; I heard it knock several times as the road climbed into the foothills of the canyon. I hoped it would get

Will wherever he was going.

"I heard they's gonna make Alaska a state soon," Will said. "Might have to git me up there some time. Have a look around."

I nodded. "Lot's of open space there for sure."

"Gold too, I heard. Jus' like California a hunderd years ago. Folks makin' claims and such, gittin' rich."

"Could be," I said. "That can still be a tough way to earn a living." I knew first hand how hard it could be to make ends meet working the land.

Will grunted in agreement. "Still, might be better'n drivin' a truck," he said with a chuckle.

He fell silent then and a few minutes later I spotted my destination up ahead. "If you don't mind dropping me off just around that bend, I'd be grateful."

He nodded and took his foot off the gas. The truck decelerated quickly, going uphill as we were.

"Thank you, Will," I said when we came to a stop. "Saved my old legs a lot of work."

He shook my hand again and said, "Well, good luck, Christophe."

I climbed down and waved to him in the side mirror. He grinned and eased the truck back into gear. With a cloud of dark smoke, Will headed west into the mountains once more.

I coughed some of the truck's exhaust from my lungs and made my way across the road to a small trail leading down the embankment to the creek, thirty feet below. I pulled out my flask and took a swig to clear my throat. Loose earth caused me to lose my balance twice, but I made it down to the water without landing on my backside. I sat on a small boulder beside the burbling creek and pulled my leather lure wallet from my pocket. I usually had better luck with dry flies, but decided that would be too much work since my main purpose was simply to drown my sorrows. I selected my Royal Coachman and tied it to the end of my line.

After setting the lure case aside on another rock, I pulled another deep swallow of whiskey and proceeded to get my fly wet. The creek was about twenty yards across at that spot and a good depth for trout. Something at the back of my mind told me it didn't really matter since I hadn't brought anything to carry fish home if I caught any.

I took another drink and told the back of my mind to shut up and mind its own business.

As things stood, I'd have plenty of time to fish since I'd lost my job the day before.

It hadn't been anything to write home about, as jobs went, but it paid for the room I rented, and a bottle of hooch now and then. Not many folks were eager to hire a sixty-year-old mechanic. Especially one who was also a drunk.

The morning sun crested the canyon wall and sudden reflections from the water dazzled my vision. The world spun and the flashes continued even after I closed my eyes. Pain shot through my left side and I staggered to the bank, dropping my pole.

Falling face first into the sand and pebbles, darkness swallowed me.

# Margot

## *July 5, 1958*

Margot sat back and checked over her notes while Christophe finished the juice she'd given him earlier. His slurred speech had been difficult to follow at first, but she eventually had acquired an ear for it and made sense of the scenes and feelings he had described.

She made a few additions to her notebook, then saw from her watch it was nearly time for lunch. Collecting her things, she stood and patted Christophe on the shoulder. "Get some rest and I'll be back this afternoon."

He gave her a weak smile and handed her the empty cup.

Margot made her exit and hurried to the institution's pharmacy to help with dispensing medications. The impersonal walls of the hallway did nothing to buoy her spirits.

She felt deeply sorry for Christophe. He certainly wasn't the typical derelict or incurable psychotic she so often came in contact with in her position. Being the newest doctor on staff — not to mention being a woman — she usually dealt with the cases offering the least hope for recovery. So many of the patients she worked with on a daily basis had no concept of, or interaction with, the environment around them. They were souls locked away within their own minds, oblivious to their bodies which continued functioning, but without purpose. Christophe, however, was obviously intelligent and able to operate adequately within society, but either the stroke, or some other malady, had caused his memory to be suppressed, leaving him abandoned in the world.

Margot was familiar with abandonment. She'd been dealing with it all her life.

While still an infant, she had been left with her grandparents in Minnesota. They had cared for her until an accident, with a piece of heavy equipment on the farm they owned, took the life of her grandfather when Margot was around two years old. Her grandmother, after several months of struggling by herself, was forced to sell the farm and turned Margot over to an orphanage in the town of Worthington, in the southwestern corner of the state.

Those bits of information were all she knew of her real family. She had never known her parents, nor why they hadn't been able to care for her — or even why her grandmother hadn't sent her back to them after her grandfather had been killed. Margot supposed they must have met with a similar ill fate.

She spent the next several years of her life moving from foster home, to foster home, until she was about nine, when an elderly couple, who had never had children of their own, had taken her in on a permanent basis.

Her time in the orphanage and foster care had taught her the only person she could truly count on in life was herself. That self-reliance had given her the strength to push herself through school and higher education, in a field where few women had ventured. Of course, that same strength and determination had made it difficult to form lasting relationships, causing more tales of abandonment and broken promises through her life.

Hal had been the first person to really accept her as she was, and not expect her to change or be something she wasn't once they began to develop feelings for one another. It had come as a surprise to Margot, and it had taken a long time for her to trust him, and the relationship, enough to move forward into something beyond simple friendship.

Margot thought about those things as she sorted pills into small paper cups for the patients. Christophe's situation bothered her because she felt there must be someone out there who cared for him, or had in the past. He'd indicated under the hypnosis that he was about sixty. Although he evidently drank, he seemed a personable sort and easy to talk to. Someone like that didn't go through a long life and not make connections of some kind along the way. Was someone looking for him? Did someone miss him? Margot didn't know the answers to those questions, but she was determined to find out.

After finishing up with the medications, she went back to her office and read through her notes, sitting in her ill-proportioned chair. Christophe had described the morning before his stroke in excellent detail, but Margot couldn't decipher any more hints of his identity, or of anyone who would be interested in his whereabouts. He apparently had lived in a rented room, somewhere in Denver, but that would be nearly impossible to track down in a city that size. She would have to delve deeper into his past to search for more substantial information.

One thing that concerned her was his reference to a "knot" in his stomach, which had sounded like a chronic problem for him. She checked through the medical reports St. Luke's had sent along, but saw no mention of any stomach disorders. Margot made a note to have Christophe's stool and urine checked for abnormalities, then selected several volumes from her bookshelves, looking for more references on hypnosis.

Before she realized it, the afternoon was gone and it was time for the evening meal. Margot returned Christophe's medical records to the front desk for filing, then went to assist the nurses with medications once again. It was a tedious and ongoing, but vital, task that Margot alternately loathed and anticipated, depending on her mood. While the meals were served, she did a walk-through, checking the patients' statistics for the day. Her stomach was rumbling by the time she finished and signed off to the night shift nurses.

Driving home, Margot thought more about Christophe. He mentioned he'd been fired from his job, which was why he had gone into the mountains to fish and drink, but his recollection hadn't revealed what his job had been. She supposed that would be as good a starting point as any for their next session. If she could track down his former employer, they would likely have some of his personal information on file.

Margot parked on the street in front of their home in the waning daylight of a long summer's day. Hal's car, a late forties Ford pickup truck, sat in their driveway. She saw the kitchen light was on and smiled as she walked past the truck. The clinking of dishes in the sink greeted her on opening the door.

"Got you workin' pretty long hours these days," Hal said from the kitchen sink.

The home they'd purchased was small, but suited their needs. The front door opened into a cozy parlor, where they kept a radio and a small black and white television across from a mismatched loveseat and high back chair. To the left, a cramped dining room led into the galley style kitchen.

"Just for the weekend," Margot replied. "All the senior staff wanted a holiday break." She joined him in next to the sink as he pulled the stopper on the drain and dried off a plate with a worn hand towel.

"There's still some tuna casserole left if you want some," he said, inclining his head toward the oven behind them. "Left it in there to stay warm."

Margot chuckled. "Liar, you left it in there so you wouldn't have to wash another dish."

Hal laughed as he set the plate in the cupboard, then raised his hands in surrender. "Guilty as charged."

Margot found a potholder and retrieved the casserole from the oven. After serving herself what remained, she set the dish in the sink to soak and carried her food to the dining room table. Hal followed and sat next to her as she ate.

"Worked on a Cadillac today," he said while she chewed. "Felt like I ought to be washin' my hands every five minutes. Never seen a car that pretty. Still, under the hood, not much different when you get right down to it."

Margot nodded, doing her best not to eat too fast even though her stomach begged for more. She knew nothing about cars, except how to drive one, but appreciated Hal keeping her company at the table. Looking up at his rugged face, she smiled, noting a grease spot on the bridge of his hooked nose. His brown eyes smiled in return.

"You have any excitement today?" he asked.

She shook her head and swallowed a bite. "Not really. Though I did find out the name of my mystery patient that came in yesterday. Christophe."

Hal's eyebrows crinkled. "Sounds foreign. He's not a Commie, is he?" he asked with a laugh.

Margot giggled at his joke. "I don't think so. I didn't find out much other than that. He seems like a pleasant person, just maybe had a run of bad luck lately. I'll try again tomorrow. See if I can uncover any more of his past."

Hal shrugged his broad shoulders and chuckled. "You dig around in people's brains like I do in a car's engine. Me? I'll take the engine. Not as many surprises."

❧

Margot sat next to Christophe's bed the next morning, notebook in her lap. The elderly man had eaten his breakfast earlier and seemed in better spirits.

"How are you feeling this morning?" she asked him.

"Not bad, I guessss."

"That's good. Do you remember our session yesterday?"

The right side of Christophe's brow furrowed. "I remembah we talked a bit. You gave me sssome juicccce."

Margot nodded. "Yes. Do you remember anything else?"

He frowned. "Not that I can think of."

She sat back, puzzled by his response. Margot had given him a command to keep the memories he'd related to her in his mind, but they evidently hadn't stayed with him. She would have to continue her research. Find out if she'd done something wrong. "We did discover your name is Christophe," she told him. "And that you were fishing in Turkey Creek when you had your stroke. Now, I'd like to take you back to the previous day. You had a job you'd been working at and if we can find out where, they may have more information about you. Maybe know your family."

Christophe nodded and focused his eyes on the gold pendant Margot pulled from her pocket.

# Christophe

*June 26, 1958*

I walked through the open gate and waved to Mike in the small, windowed booth marking the entrance to the junkyard. He half-heartedly waved back, busy with paperwork, or, more likely, staring at the pictures in a girlie magazine.

Gravel crunched under my feet and the morning sun warmed my back with the promise of a hot day ahead.

I made my way to the imposing, open metal building Mike used to inspect and tear apart the vehicles that came into his possession at the yard. I worked with two or three other men, depending on the day, checking over cars and trucks. Once in a while, a salvage came in that didn't require much effort to fix up. We'd take care of those and Mike sold them to some used car lot, down the road a piece.

Melvin was already there, his feet sticking out from under a late thirties Chevy, by the look of it. I knew it was him from the mismatched pair of cowboy boots he wore.

"Morning, Mel," I said.

A grunt came in reply from beneath the car. The body was

rusted in a few spots, but appeared to be in decent shape.

"Any hope for this one?" I asked him.

"Nah," Mel said. "Transmission's all tore up. I'm just pulling all the fluids so the thing don't leak everywhere in the yard."

I nodded, even though Mel couldn't see me, and went to the workbench to pick up a rag and a pan to help him.

A short time later, just as Mel and I were finishing up, Ralph shuffled in. He smiled lopsidedly when he saw me. Ralph was simple, with overly wide-set eyes and a shock of blonde hair that looked as if it hadn't seen a comb in months. He was also strong as an ox and not afraid of getting his hands dirty, so Mike kept him around. Ralph helped us push the Chevy into the yard where the crane operator would pick it up and find a permanent home for it, after we removed the hubcaps and tires.

We checked over four more cars through the day, one of which Mel and I thought we might be able to get running again with some work. The afternoon heat was stifling, but one of the nice waitresses from the diner across the street came and brought the three of us some ice water. We thanked her and sat in the dirt on the shady side of the garage building.

I rubbed the cold glass against my forehead, letting the condensation dribble down my face. Ralph watched me and mimicked the gesture. He let out a short burst of laughter a moment later, taking pleasure in the brief respite from the heat.

I took a deep drink, grateful for the break, and sucked on a piece of ice. My joints, and especially my hips, did better when it was warm, but I didn't enjoy being soaked in sweat. Denver had a reputation of being cold and snowy, since it's near the mountains, but it got quite hot in the summertime.

A shadow advanced past the edge of the building. "Mel! Christophe!" Mike shouted before coming around the corner. "There you are! I don't pay you fellas to sit around all day. Christophe, I got a customer needs some help."

I sighed and drained the rest of my water. Handing the glass to Ralph, I said, "Take these back to the diner across the way and tell them, 'Thank you.' Okay, Ralph?"

The big man grinned at me and nodded his oversized head.

I levered myself up and followed Mike back to the booth beside the entrance. A young man stood there, fidgeting with impatience. He wore a plain shirt and blue jeans, rolled up at the cuffs. His slicked-back hair shone in the sun.

Mike addressed the youngster. "Christophe here'll help you."

The young man looked me up and down quickly. "I need a grill for a '53 Ford coupe, Pops. You got one of them?"

I nodded. "We should. Follow me."

Mike rarely helped folks search through the yard. He said it was because he didn't want to leave the booth empty — like it might fly away if he weren't sitting in it — but mostly he was just lazy. Mel had a quick temper and Ralph was, well, Ralph, so the job fell to me most of the time.

A boom sounded out in the yard, from the crane dropping a car onto its designated pile. I must have flinched because the kid asked, "You okay, Pops?"

I nodded and continued on. There were a lot of noises in the yard that made me jumpy. I could generally ignore them in the garage, but they were louder and more frequent as you got into the yard itself. I didn't like going out there.

The Fords, of course, were stacked at the far end of the property.

Out of the corner of my eye, I saw another car rising in the air at the end of the crane's cable. I came to a stop before two rows of vehicles, each stacked over eight feet high. "Down there," I pointed. "About half way, you should find one."

The youth walked ahead a few steps, then turned around. "Ain't you gonna help me?"

I let out a breath and swallowed, my throat already dry again from the dust and heat. The two lines of junkers seemed to stretch on forever. As I stepped forward, the alley we walked in shrank, closing in on me.

Another boom went off and a flowery smell teased my nose, causing the knot in my gut to flare in pain. Cracks and pops rattled above my head and I heard shouts from men somewhere in the distance.

The next thing I knew, I was rolling on the ground with another body.

"Get off me old man! What is wrong with you?"

The youngster scrambled out from underneath me and got to his feet. I looked up at him, unsure of what had happened, or even where I was.

He started to say something else, then simply turned and ran.

I shook my head, trying to recall what I had done, but found nothing. My Hole had claimed me, once again. Slowly, I got to my feet and dusted myself off. Scared and disgusted, I began walking back to the garage.

Mike met me halfway there. "What the hell happened!?"

"I don't know."

"Kid said you jumped him, yelling, 'Masks!' or something."

I stared back at Mike. His face was red from exertion and anger. "I don't know," I said again. "I don't remember."

Mike looked at me in disbelief. "Go home, Christophe. Don't come back. I can't have some lunatic scaring off the customers like that."

I sighed and dropped my head. Mike's boots crunched through the gravel as he walked away. I felt something wet slide down my cheek and I wondered if I would ever be able to escape the Hole.

# Margot

## *July 6, 1958*

**S**hocked by Christophe's narrative, Margot brought him out of the trance as quickly as she dared. Clearly, something deeper was involved with Christophe's memory loss than side effects from his stroke.

He seemed unaffected by the experience, other than having developed a thirst from so much talking. He sipped from a cup of water while Margot collected her thoughts.

The "Hole" he'd spoken of sounded like a missing, or repressed, memory. She had heard of cases where something so horrific or traumatic had happened to a patient, their mind blocked out the event as a mechanism for dealing with the pain and mental anguish. Occasionally, the memory would resurface, causing the patient to lose their grip on the real world and become immersed in the remembered occurrence.

Freud had discussed repressed memory at length, but, as with much of his work, it centered on a sexual theme. Margot didn't believe Christophe's episode had been sexual in nature. It sounded as if the loud noises of the junkyard, and possibly a feeling of claustrophobia from the stacks of cars surrounding him, had triggered it.

Regardless, Margot at least felt she had a place to start looking for people who knew Christophe. Even though he hadn't revealed a name for the business, how many junkyards could there be in Denver? Plus, she had the name of the owner, or at least the person in charge of the place: Mike.

Buoyed by the discoveries, her routine tasks for the rest of the day went fast and smooth. Tomorrow, the regular staff would be back and she was due to have the day after that, Tuesday, off. Margot was already planning a trip up to Denver to investigate Christophe's memories.

When she arrived home that night, Hal surprised her by taking her out to dinner and a movie.

"What's the occasion?" Margot asked as he rushed her out the door to the car.

"Occasion? Why does there have to be an 'occasion' for a man to take his wife out on the town?"

Margot giggled. "Why indeed!" Hal opened the car door and she tucked her hastily donned dress under her legs as she got in.

They ate a simple meal at one of their favorite coffee houses, then rushed to the theater to catch *The Sheepman*, with Glenn Ford and Shirley MacLaine. The movie was funny — Margot enjoyed Ford's wry smile and sense of humor — and she and Hal arrived home full of laughter. Hal was no Cyrano de Bergerac, but Margot had never been one for that traditional type of romance. The night was perfect, and carried on long after the lights went out.

Margot arrived at work the next morning with a bounce in her step, in contrast to many who seemed in slow motion after their long weekend away. Margot smiled at Edith and picked up a handful of notes from her mail cubby.

"Dr. Randolph has scheduled a staff meeting at ten," Edith said. "But he would like to see you before then, if possible."

Margot knew the "if possible" had been Edith's addition. Dr. Alfred Randolph lorded over the institution as if it were his own and not the State of Colorado's. "Thank you, Edith," she said and walked down the hall toward her office.

Once inside, she stowed her purse in a desk drawer and glanced through the notes she'd picked up. Most were status reports on her patients from the night shift. No changes, everything status quo — the usual. One, however, was from Christophe, written by one of the nurses judging from the handwriting, thanking Margot for her care and the work she'd done so far. It brought another smile to her face and she folded it neatly before sliding it in the pocket of her lab coat.

Dr. Randolph's office sat in the front corner of the building, with windows that looked out to the west and south. Margot didn't begrudge him the windows. Likely the office was an oven in the afternoon this time of year, but since Dr. Randolph was usually out golfing at those times, she doubted he'd ever experienced that uncomfortable heat.

Margot knocked lightly on the door before entering. Dr.

Randolph sat behind his oversized mahogany desk scrutinizing an open file in front of him. The rest of the expansive slab of polished wood was largely empty, with the exceptions of a letter opener, a silver pencil holder, and a posed family photo encased in an engraved frame.

"Have a seat, please, Dr. Braun," he said without looking up.

Margot stepped in and sat on the edge of one of the two high backed chairs facing his desk. She always felt like she was back in med school, sitting in those chairs, with Dr. Randolph playing the part of an unhappy dean. His close-cropped haircut harkened back to his military days, but it currently sported much more salt than pepper.

"I understand we had a new guest arrive from St. Luke's," he said, eyes still focused on the file.

Margot nodded. Dr. Randolph always referred to the patients as "guests," even though the majority of them would never be allowed to leave the facility. "Yes, sir. He had a stroke, which he was treated for at St. Luke's, but it was accompanied by memory loss and no family stepped forward to claim him."

"I see here you've attempted to resurrect his memory through hypnosis?"

She nodded again. "Yes, I've read some recent articles where that treatment has proven effective."

He looked up at last and raised a dark eyebrow. "And has your implementation of that treatment been effective in this case?"

Margot felt her cheeks color in spite of her best efforts to maintain her composure. "I believe so, sir." Dr. Randolph was in his late fifties and very much an old school psychiatrist. Anything out of the ordinary he viewed with the same respect as mummery or snake oil. "In our session yesterday he described his former workplace to me, enough so that I plan to make a trip to Denver on my day off tomorrow to follow up on it."

Dr. Randolph's lips thinned, ever so slightly. "Very well. You may continue with your efforts as long as progress is made. I expect, however, your care and attention for the other guests under your supervision to remain at the highest level."

"Of course, sir."

"Carry on."

Margot gratefully rose from the chair and walked to the door.

"Ah, Dr. Braun?" he said as she reached for the handle.

She turned back. "Yes?"

"The hospital, of course, cannot pay for any expenses in relation to your outing tomorrow, you understand?"

Margot suppressed a sardonic smile. "Of course, sir," she said and left the office, shutting the door only slightly harder than necessary.

The rest of her day was mercifully uneventful. She managed to find time to briefly thank Christophe for his note and let him know she would be traveling to Denver the next day to look into what they had learned. He thanked her again and she left work that evening with a sense of purpose and renewed energy.

# Margot

*July 8, 1958*

**H**aving left home shortly before six, Margot arrived in Denver with most of the morning still ahead of her. She stopped at a gas station on her way into the city and found a pay phone while the attendants filled up the tank and washed the windows.

The phone book was massive compared to Pueblo's and her heart sank when she thumbed through to the section labeled "junkyards." Margot counted nearly thirty listings! With a sigh, she pulled a notebook from her purse and began writing down addresses and phone numbers. She soon realized, much to her relief, that most of the addresses were relatively close together near downtown. Her nearly impossible task was downgraded to incredibly difficult.

Margot paid for her gas and purchased a city map before pulling out into the busy morning traffic.

Although Pueblo was not what she considered a "small" town, it was dwarfed by Denver. Margot had visited, and lived in places like Chicago, St. Louis, and the Twin Cities, but she'd spent most of her life in small to mid-sized towns. The sheer volume of cars on the road daunted her, never mind that she was unsure of where she was going.

By the time she parked her car across the street from "Joe's Junk," Margot was quite discouraged. It was past noon and she'd already visited eleven of the addresses from her list with no luck. She grabbed her purse from the passenger seat and stepped out of the car. Sounds of heavy machinery filled the air and the heat coming off the pavement gave her pause to wish for a drink of water. I'll take a break after I check this one, she decided.

The large lot was fenced along the street but for an open gravel driveway leading into the yard itself. Immediately to the right of the entrance, she saw a small shack with an open door and window.

"Hello?" Margot called toward the small structure as she walked closer.

A middle-aged man with dark brown hair poked his head out the window. His eyes widened when they landed on Margot and a smile spread across his face. "Hello! How can I help you?"

Margot's stomach turned and she put a hand to her mouth. Hunger and the creepy feeling she got from the man in front of her made a bad combination. "Excuse me, but can you tell me if a man named Christophe used to work here?"

The man's expression soured. "Used to, yeah. Fired him a week or two ago."

Margot filled with excitement. "Really? You must be Mike then!"

His brow creased in suspicion. "Who wants to know?"

"I'm Dr. Margot Braun," she said, holding out her hand. "I'd like to ask you a few questions about Christophe, with your permission."

He hesitated, then shook her hand. "Yeah, I'm Mike. Boy, that guy had all the luck with the dames."

"Pardon me?"

"Christophe. Haven't seen him since he left. Don't know much about him really. Why you looking for him?"

"Oh, I'm not. He had a stroke and suffered some memory loss. I'm trying to find some family of his."

Mike's eyebrows rose. "Hm. Don't recall him ever talking about any family."

"Can you at least tell me his last name?"

"Don't know that either. We're, uh, kind of informal around here. I pay the boys in cash at the end of each day. Who'd you say you were with?"

Margot's spirits sank a bit. Now that she'd found him, she realized Mike wasn't going to be as much help as she'd hoped. Still, it proved the memories Christophe had related weren't simply fantasy. "I'm with the State Hospital in Pueblo. No one's in any trouble. I just want to find someone with a connection to Christophe to help him regain his memory."

Mike seemed skeptical. "I don't think I can be of much help to you."

Margot pulled the notebook from her purse and flipped through it. "What about … Mel? Or Ralph? Are they here?"

"Yeah," Mike said after a pause. "Probably out back of the shop having a bite of lunch, but I don't think they'll know much more about him."

"Mind if I talk with them?"

"Nah, I guess not. But not too long, they got work to do."

Margot nodded and smiled in thanks. The metal-framed building Christophe had described was off to her left. She headed for it, not for the first time that day wishing she'd worn flats instead of the modest heels she'd chosen. Her feet were unsteady in the gravel. She rounded the corner into the shade and saw two men sitting on the ground with their backs to the wall of the shop, quietly eating sandwiches.

"Excuse me, I'm sorry to bother you."

Both men looked up at her, but with very different expressions. The one she was sure was Ralph smiled awkwardly at her with a mouth full of crooked teeth. Mel, on the other hand, scowled at the interruption of his lunch.

"I wanted to ask you about Christophe. He used to work with you?"

Ralph's smile broadened, but he didn't respond otherwise. Mel said, "Yeah, 'til he went crazy on some kid."

"What happened?"

"Don't know much but what Mike said. Christophe was helping this kid find a part back in the yard, then he tackled him for some reason. Scared the kid half to death I guess."

"Do you know if Christophe had any family around?"

Mel shook his head. "Not that I ever heard. But we don't

have time for tongue wagging around here." He cocked his head. "Check over at the diner. One of them waitresses was sweet on him I think."

Ralph smiled again.

"What about you, Ralph? Did you know Christophe well?" Margot asked.

"Lady, Ralph don't talk," Mel said. "He ain't all there, if you know what I mean."

She nodded. "I do. But it never hurts to ask."

Mel scoffed at her and said, "I got a oil pan needs draining, if you'll excuse me."

Margot smiled at Ralph and turned back toward the entrance to the yard. She managed to walk back to the street without tripping in the gravel and waved to Mike on her way out. She spied the diner not far from where she'd parked. It would be good to sit and get out of the heat for a while.

Blessedly, the place was air-conditioned and Margot blew a sigh of relief once inside. The restaurant was mostly full, with the buzz of many conversations and clinks of silverware against dishes. A waitress flashed by with an armload of plates. "Sit wherever you like, Darlin'," she said as she passed.

Margot chose an empty booth next to the front window with a view of the junkyard and her car. Her visit had been tantalizing, but had produced little in the way of real information. She felt as if she were chasing shadows. Looking across the street, she envisioned Christophe there, moving amongst the heaps of scrap.

"Did you need a menu, Darlin'?"

The waitress pulled Margot from her reverie. The woman was perhaps in her mid-forties, with auburn hair, neatly pulled up in a bun. She wore a light blue dress with a white apron tied around her waist, and the name "Irene" was embroidered above her left breast.

"Do you have a BLT?" Margot asked.

"We sure do. What would you like to drink?"

"Oh, just some water for now," Margot said with a smile.

Irene smiled back, jotting the order on her pad. "I'll get this right in for you."

A boom from across the street startled Margot, causing her heart to race. Irene chuckled. "It's all right," she said, putting a hand on Margot's shoulder. "Jeff must be back from his lunch. He runs the crane at the yard across the way. You get used to the noise after a while." With that, Irene left to turn in Margot's order.

For herself, Margot wasn't convinced she could get used to something like that. It had seemed almost like cannon fire. She watched the yard and saw the crane lifting a car into the air and subsequently dropping it onto a pile of scrap with a loud crash. The window next to her even vibrated slightly in sympathy. Christophe had mentioned the sounds of the yard making him anxious and Margot could understand why. It reminded her of some of the World War II newsreels she'd seen in the movie theater, with the allied big guns firing on enemy troops.

A short time later, Irene arrived with her sandwich and a

glass of ice water. Margot's stomach rumbled in anticipation. "Anything else I can get for you?"

"Just a question actually," Margot said. "You mentioned you knew the crane operator. Did you also know a man named Christophe who worked over there?"

Irene's smile faltered and she gave Margot a small nod. "I did. But he's been gone for almost two weeks. Why? Do you know him? Do you know where he went?"

Margot nodded in return. "He had a stroke, but he's recovering. However, he's also suffered some severe memory loss and I'm trying to piece together his life. Find out if he has any family."

"Who are you?" Irene asked.

Margot chuckled and held out her hand. "I'm sorry, my name's Margot Braun. I'm a doctor who's working with Christophe."

Irene took her hand and smiled with relief. "Oh! Nice to meet you Dr. Braun."

"Margot, please."

"Irene!" a husky voice shouted from the kitchen. "Order's up!"

Irene sighed. "I gotta get back to work, but I'll be back."

Margot turned her attention to the sandwich and dug in with gusto. The bacon was crispy, just like she liked it, and the tomato was full of flavor. She savored every bite, but it wasn't long before her plate held nothing but crumbs.

Several of the other customers had finished their meals in

the meantime and the diner quieted, though the occasional crash still sounded from the junkyard. Irene appeared once more and removed the empty plate.

"What would you like for dessert? We have apple, cherry, and rhubarb pie."

"Oh, goodness. I don't think I need any," Margot said.

Irene chuckled. "None of us ever need any, Darlin', but we have it just the same. My treat, for helping Christophe."

Margot laughed. "All right. Apple then, please."

"Coffee?"

"Yes, please."

"Coming right up," Irene said with a grin.

She soon returned with a generous slice of pie accompanied by a dollop of vanilla ice cream, and a cup of coffee. "Cream or sugar?"

Margot shook her head. "I drank straight from the pot in college. Only way to get through."

Irene laughed, then her smile faded. "You did say Christophe was all right, didn't you?"

Margot nodded while taking a sip of coffee. "Do you have time to sit?"

Irene glanced back at the kitchen, then sat on the corner of the booth seat. "I didn't know him that well, but I would have liked to. He came in once in a while after work and had dinner, or just a piece of pie — he liked the cherry — and we'd have a chat sometimes."

"Do you know if he had any family around?"

Irene shook her head. "He never talked about anyone. But I didn't know him that long. He only started working in the yard about three months ago."

Margot sighed. *More dead ends.* "Do you know where he lived? Or if he had any other friends?"

"There's a boarding house a few blocks from here, on Madison." Irene's cheeks colored lightly. "I walked him there a couple of times after my shift. But he never let me come up. He was too proud I think, didn't want me to see the conditions he was living in." She sighed. "I lost my Bernard in the Big One. It was hard, but I raised our boy, Jack, myself after that. Now, he's been gone a couple years — enlisted and he's building bridges or some thing and I haven't seen him but a couple of times — and a woman gets lonely, you know? I knew Christophe was older, but he had such life in him, and he treated people right. Like that poor slow boy at the yard — Ralph, I think his name is — Christophe never talked down to him, or called him names." Irene blushed again. "Listen to me! Sitting here talking your ear off and not even answering your questions!"

Margot laughed. "It's all right. I'm eager to learn anything about him I can. Could you show me where the boarding house is? I'm from Pueblo and not very familiar with Denver."

Irene looked up at a clock on the wall. "I'm off in about an hour if you care to wait."

"That should be fine. It'll give me time to work through this pie!"

The pie was delicious and before she knew it, Margot's plate was empty. She thought some more about what she'd learned of Christophe. The preliminary information indicated a man with few emotional ties, and one who wanted to keep it that way. Something in his past had caused him to close himself off from the world, to live the life of a drifter. Unfortunately, Margot was no closer to knowing what had been the catalyst for that regression.

Irene joined her after changing out of her waitressing uniform at the end of her shift. She wore an ivory-colored summer dress with teal accents. "Shall we go?" she asked Margot.

"Do you have a car?"

"I usually walk when it's nice and I'm not working late. I don't live far."

"I see," Margot said with a smile. She counted out the money to pay her check and handed it to the young woman working the till. Dry July heat blasted them as they walked out the door. Margot hadn't realized how pleasant the air-conditioned restaurant had been.

She showed Irene to her car and, after burning her fingers on the ignition, Margot plucked a handkerchief from her purse so she could hold onto the steering wheel in the stifling heat. Once they got moving with the windows down, it wasn't quite as bad.

Irene directed her to the proper street, then she said, "I know I keep asking this, but is Christophe all right? I mean you said he had a stroke …"

Margot spared her a glance, concentrating on the road. "He's stable, as far as we can tell, but the stroke partially paralyzed the left side of his body. He can walk, but only with help."

Irene bowed her head briefly. "I'm sorry. It must be killing him — to be like that, I mean. He was so active. Oh! It's right up here."

Margot drove a bit farther along the street and found a parking spot. The house Irene had pointed out was a large two-story, with a wrap around porch and in bad need of a paint job. The steps leading up to the front double doors had been crudely supported with the odd piece of wood here and there, but still looked as if they may collapse at any moment. Margot sighed, then gingerly climbed up and knocked at the door.

"It's open!" a gravely voice shouted from inside.

The parlor area Margot and Irene stepped into looked no better than the outside of the house. Two overstuffed chairs sat to the left of the doorway, flanking a small table that supported a lamp with a shade yellowed from age and smoke. The chairs had been reupholstered a number of times by the look of them, and they were overdue for another treatment. The hardwood floor creaked loudly and Margot coughed involuntarily from the cigarette smoke hanging heavily in the room.

"I'm full up," the same voice from earlier said. To Margot's right, a grizzled woman sat behind a worn, metal desk, adding steadily to the smoke in the room. "Don't rent to women no how."

Margot cleared her throat. "We're not looking for a room, ma'am. Did you have a boarder here by the name of Christophe?"

The woman took another puff from her cigarette. "Maybe.

Who wants to know?"

"I'm Dr. Margot Braun, and this is a friend of mine, Irene. Christophe was injured and has suffered some memory loss. I'm trying to find out if he has any family or relations around."

After eyeing Margot and Irene, the woman stamped out her cigarette in an already full ashtray at the edge of the desk. "He hasn't been here for about two weeks. But I guess you know that. Anyway, he was by himself, far as I could tell. When he didn't show up after a week, I cleaned out the room."

"Do you still have his belongings?"

"Nope. Sold what I could. Trashed the rest. Wasn't much 'cept some old clothes really."

Disappointed, Margot asked, "Can we see the room?"

The old woman shook her head. "Rented it out two days ago. I cleaned it out right good. Weren't nothin' else in there."

Considering the condition of the building, Margot doubted the woman's cleaning skills. Nevertheless, she had come to another dead end. "Do you have any payment records I might look at? Something with his last name at least?"

"Sorry. I run strictly cash only here. Don't keep records," she said, lighting another cigarette and taking a deep drag.

"All right," Margot said. "Thank you for your time."

Irene followed Margot out the door and into the afternoon sunshine. "What a pleasant old coot," Irene said with a chuckle.

Margot laughed. "She wasn't very helpful. Though, I got the feeling she was being honest. Still, all this does is put me nearly back at square one."

"How did you know to come looking here?"

Margot opened her car door. "I placed him under hypnosis. He relayed some memories to me that his conscious mind had forgotten, or suppressed. At least I know the technique works. Everything he told me seems to have been accurate."

"I wish I could help more."

"He never mentioned any family at all to you?"

Irene shook her head. "He really didn't talk much. He let me do all the gum flappin'," she said with a laugh. "He's a real good listener."

Margot nodded, then she found her notebook and tore out a page after she'd scribbled some information. "Here's my telephone number, and the address of the hospital in Pueblo. If you ever think of something, or have a question, please feel free to contact me."

Irene took the paper with a smile. "I will. Thank you for helping him."

"Can I give you a lift home?"

"No. I believe I'll walk. I need some time to think."

"All right. Take care of yourself. It was nice meeting you." Margot said.

"Likewise."

Standing beside her car, Margot watched Irene walk up the street and turn right at the corner. It was obvious Christophe had had an effect on the woman. Margot couldn't believe he'd gone through the rest of his life without affecting others in a similar fashion. She just had to find them.

# Margot

*July 9, 1958*

Margot's drive home had been uneventful and she'd lain awake deep into the night, pondering her options.

She knew many cases of mental trauma were the result of war and combat. Christophe was certainly too old to have actively participated in the Korean conflict, and probably World War II as well, but Margot still decided to try that time period in their next session. Even if he hadn't been in the war, she might be able to uncover something else — some other clue to his life from before.

Her mind still buzzing with possibilities, Margot arrived at the hospital in the morning and smiled at Edith on her way through the lobby.

"Dr. Braun?" the elderly woman called to her.

Margot stopped, then remembered she should check her message cubby. "Yes?"

"Dr. Randolph asked to see you when you came in."

Margot sighed. She was eager to visit with Christophe. "All right. Thank you, Edith."

After dropping her purse and the few messages she'd retrieved off in her office, Margot went to see Dr. Randolph. She rapped her knuckles on the door and walked in.

"Dr. Braun, thank you for coming. How was your trip yesterday?"

Margot sat in one of the chairs facing his desk, as was expected. "It was interesting. It took some leg work, but I did find Christophe's former place of employment and a few people that knew him."

Dr. Randolph raised an eyebrow slightly. "I see. And were you able to contact any family?"

"No. But the memories retrieved through the hypnosis proved accurate. I think with some more time, I can get him to recall some more concrete —"

Dr. Randolph held up a hand. "I had a talk with your Mr. Doe yesterday. I'm not convinced he's been truthful about his amnesia."

"What?"

"I've never seen a case where memory loss was that pervasive. Even in cases of stroke."

"I don't think the memory loss is entirely due to the stroke," Margot said. "He's mentioned what he calls a 'Hole' in his thoughts during the hypnosis. I think he suffered some form of trauma in his past, and the stroke has exacerbated the problem."

Dr. Randolph tapped a pen lightly on his desk and scowled. "Very well. Continue your work, your current patient load permitting, but I want to see some definitive results within a week."

"Yes, sir."

"If you can't produce some family, or at least some verifiable identity, I'll have to turn him over to Dr. Tate's care."

Margot flinched inwardly. Dr. Tate was notoriously unforgiving with his charges. Although the practice had fallen out of favor in recent years, Margot knew Dr. Tate had performed several lobotomies in the past. She didn't believe he would recommend such a radical procedure in Christophe's case, but Tate's willingness to still consider it for some of their more troublesome patients gave her chills. "I'm sure that won't be necessary," she said.

"I sincerely hope not, Dr. Braun. I do believe, however, Mr. Doe has aroused some maternal emotions in you that, when tempered, are beneficial to our profession, but can cause you to become misguided in some cases."

She opened her mouth to respond, then thought better of it. An argument of gender was one she would never win with Dr. Randolph. It would only infuriate her, and consequently reinforce his opinion that women were too emotional to perform clinical work. Margot composed herself and stood. "If there's nothing else, I have a busy schedule to see to."

Dr. Randolph gave her a thin smile and indicated the door. "Of course."

She turned and left his office, managing to keep a lid on her temper — barely. Margot took solace in the fact she was there for the patients, not the staff. It would be a chilly day in hell before Dr. Randolph, and others like him, would admit a woman could perform their job — or any job short of cooking and cleaning — as well as a man. The patients she worked with, however, didn't care that their doctor was a woman.

Then again, most of her patients might not have been aware the sky was blue either.

Disgusted with her destructive train of thought, she busied herself with her morning routine. She checked up on all of her patients and visited with the nurses and orderlies, checking over their notes from the day before when she'd been in Denver. She adjusted medication dosages for two of the patients and made notes in their files. With all that completed, Margot allowed herself to relax. Whether intending to or not, Dr. Randolph always knew how to get her all stirred up.

Jangled nerves settled, she stopped by the kitchen for some fruit juice before arriving at Christophe's door. His face lit up when she walked in — even the droopy left side appeared to be making an effort to smile.

"Dr. Braun! I'm ssso glad to ssssee you."

"You're looking chipper today, Christophe," Margot answered with a smile of her own and set the juice on the table before taking a seat beside the bed.

"How wasss your trip?"

Margot had been unsure what to tell him, not knowing how he would react. She supposed he would be disappointed about not finding any family, as she was herself, but she hoped he would see the bright side and realize they were making progress with the hypnosis. She decided to lay it all out and see if any of the memories had stayed with him. "It took some time, but I was able to find the junkyard where you used to work. The people there remembered you, but had little other information. It seems you were a bit of a recluse."

His right eye dropped for a moment, then he looked at her again. "Sssthank you for trying, Dr. Braun. It wasss a lot to hope for I guesssss."

She patted his arm. "You didn't let me finish. Do you remember a waitress named Irene?"

Christophe's brow scrunched as he searched his battered memory. At last he sighed. "No. Nothing."

Margot secretly joined in his sigh. She had held a faint hope Irene would spark some recollection. "Well she certainly remembers you! She works in the restaurant across the street from the junkyard and it seems the two of you were good friends."

"I wisssh I could remembah."

She searched his eyes and thought of Dr. Randolph. Margot could find no hint of deceit in Christophe. His pain and anguish were genuine. "Well, the good news, in my mind at least, is that we know the hypnosis is working. The memories you related to me checked out one hundred percent, so now, the trick is finding some that will lead us to your family."

Christophe struggled to sit up higher. Margot helped him and propped the pillow behind his back. "What sssshould we try?"

"Do you think you might have been a soldier? Or fought in a war?"

He paused, searching his mind again. "Maybe. I don't know. It ssssoundss right. I guessss."

"Okay. I'd like to start with some time around World War II, in the mid forties. Just relax and let your thoughts drift …"

# Christophe

## *September 9, 1946*

**A** scream from the front room split my head and made me choke on the coffee I'd just swallowed.

"Mine!" the shrill voice insisted.

"It's not yours!" Frank, my nine-year-old stepson asserted.

"Mine!" Misty, my daughter, had turned two during the summer and had recently discovered the concept of ownership. She was still fuzzy on its finer points.

"Frank," my wife, Laura, called from the bedroom. "Just let her have it, whatever it is." Peace and quiet usually went hand in hand. Laura was more interested in quiet.

"But, Mom! It's my ruler I need for school! I'm gonna be late!"

On hearing this, I set my coffee cup on the table and walked into the front room. Misty sat on a rug in the middle, fiercely clutching her newest possession. Frank, red-faced, loomed over her with murder in his eyes.

"Calm down," I said and knelt next to Misty on the floor. She eyed me suspiciously and turned her body away, protecting her prize. "Misty, the ruler is not yours. It belongs to Frank. Would you give it back to him, please?"

"Mine!" Misty replied with only slightly less volume than before.

I always tried to give folks a chance to be reasonable before I became cross. "Misty, I'm asking one last time before I give you a paddlin'. Give Frank his ruler."

The paddlin' part caught her attention and she considered her options. Reluctantly, she handed over the ruler.

Frank snatched it away, sliding it in between the two books he carried in a strap. Misty took offense at the rough treatment and tears welled up in her eyes. "Thank you, Misty," I said, pointedly looking at Frank.

He caught my hint, but instead asked, "Why should I thank her when she stole it in the first place?"

"Because it's the polite thing to do and she's only two. She's still learning right from wrong."

"You always take her side, Christophe," Frank said, jutting out his chin. He knew I didn't like him calling me by name and did it just to get a rise out of me.

I matched his look and said, "We can discuss this later. Don't you need to get going?"

Frank averted his eyes. "Yeah. 'Bye, Mom!"

"Have a good day!" Laura replied from the back of the house.

Frank slung the books over his shoulder, slamming the door behind him as he ran outside. From the window, I watched him sprint down the sidewalk to the corner, where he met two of his friends. I knew the boys were troublemakers and grew more disappointed in Frank. He was falling in with the wrong crowd, and listening to me less and less. Laura refused to believe he was anything but an angel and thought any discipline should come from me anyway. Frank had become more obstinate since Misty's arrival and I'd lost count of the times I'd heard, "You're not my dad. Why should I listen to you?"

I glanced back down at Misty and saw her toddling over to the bookshelf. I scooped her up before she could cause any damage. She squealed in frustration and an unpleasant smell reached my nose as I brought her close.

"You, young lady, are in need of a change."

Passing the bathroom as I moved through the short hallway with a squirming Misty in my arms, I saw Laura staring into the mirror, putting on makeup. "You don't need that stuff," I called back to her. I set Misty down on the changing table, which she was quickly growing out of, in our bedroom.

"Oh, yes I do," Laura said.

I shook my head and went about the business of putting a clean diaper on my daughter. Sometimes I wondered what in the world I was doing. Here I was, nearly fifty years old, just starting a family. I'd be in my sixties before Misty would be finished with school.

As I fastened the second pin, Misty looked up at me with a serene expression. She was certainly her mother's child, with her soft, curly brown hair and dark eyes. Those eyes narrowed and a crinkle of concentration appeared on her smooth forehead.

"No," I said, realizing the source of her look. "I just changed you!"

Misty ignored my plea and did her business cheerfully in the clean diaper.

"We have to start your toilet training," I said to her, reaching for another fresh diaper and washcloth.

"I don't think she's ready yet," Laura said from behind me. "Frank took a while, too."

I turned to look at her while I kept a hand on Misty's belly to keep her from rolling off the table. Laura had gone heavy with the makeup, much to my displeasure, but then I saw the reason why. "What happened to your eye?" Her right eye was swollen and discolored, even through all the cosmetics.

She turned away, then shouldered me aside and took over Misty's changing. "You happened, Christophe."

"I happened?"

"You had another nightmare last night. I tried to calm you down so you wouldn't wake the baby, then you gave me this," she said, pointing to her eye.

"I hit you?"

"Yes. And ..."

"And, what?" The knot in my stomach clenched painfully. I often had nightmares, but never remembered them when I woke.

Laura looked up from Misty's diaper. "Who is she, Christophe?"

Perplexed, I asked, "Who is who?"

"You called out a woman's name last night: Sylvie. Who is she?"

An indistinct image flashed before me, mixing with the face of my wife before me. "I don't know. I don't know anyone by that name."

Laura stared at me a second more, then turned her attention back to Misty. "I don't think I believe you," she said quietly.

My Hole had forced its way into my life once again. I struggled to recall the face I'd seen moments before, but nothing came. "Laura, I've told you there's a big chunk of my life that's gone. I don't remember. It's possible I knew someone by that name before, but I don't remember them now."

"I've seen the way the women look at you when we go shopping, or go out. The way I looked at you when we first met." She trailed off, then began again. "You work so many late hours. I don't know what to think."

"That's just the schedule Rob has me on." I worked at a service station a few blocks from the house, doing repair work and helping customers. Most days he had me on from noon until nine or so. "I thought you liked me working late so you could work and do your things in the mornings without the kids." Laura worked part time at a small five and dime store nearby for some extra money. On mornings she didn't work, she ran errands or cleaned house while I took care of Misty.

"I know," she said. "I thought I did too. I just don't know anymore. Your nightmares are getting worse. A lot worse, Christophe. And I'm scared because you don't remember anything after you wake up. It's like I'm sleeping with a totally different person." She finished pinning Misty's diaper and set her in her crib next to our bed. A tear fell away from Laura's cheek and she wiped her eye with the back of her hand. "Ugh! Now I've made a mess of my face," she lamented and retreated to the bathroom.

I stood quietly, having no way to respond. I could ignore the Hole sometimes, but having almost a decade of life missing from my memory often proved difficult to work around. I desperately wanted to remember; yet, I was frightened of what was hidden in the Hole.

Laura made a disgusted noise and I heard the sound of something hard clattering in the sink. "I have to go," she said and hurried out the front door.

I spent the rest of the morning making sure Misty stayed out of trouble and made a feeble attempt at getting her to use the toilet. Most of the time I wrestled with my fractured mind with no result.

Laura returned barely in time for me to make it to work. I grabbed my lunch pail and moved to give her a kiss, but she shied away. Several responses — few of them pleasant — passed through my thoughts, but I remained silent, for better or worse.

I jogged most of the seven blocks to be sure I'd arrive on time, and my belly and joints made it very clear they weren't happy about it. Rob smiled and waved at me from behind the counter inside where cans of oil and other items were stacked for sale. I returned the wave and went into the garage to slip on my set of blue coveralls. Jimmy, a kid fresh out of high school, sat on a barrel twiddling his thumbs, impatiently waiting for something to do. The pumps outside were clear of cars.

"Been busy today?" I asked Jimmy as I buttoned myself up.

"On and off. You know how it is."

Indeed it was rare to have a steady stream of traffic. Customers generally came in groups. Some day, some smart person might figure out why it happened that way.

I began checking over the workbench, as was my habit, making sure the tools were placed where they should be. Two cars pulled up to the pumps and Jimmy hopped off his barrel and jogged over to pump gas. I followed him out, stuffing a rag in my pocket, to check under the hoods.

The first car was a late thirties Ford. Its engine was running rough as it pulled in and the driver shut it off. I lifted the hood and noticed some oil seepage on one side.

I poked my head around and called to the driver, a heavyset man in an ill-fitting suit and tie. "Sir, looks like you've got a bad seal. Might need a new gasket or two."

The man scowled and leaned his head out the window. "I don't have time to horse around with that. I'm late for a meeting. I'm sure it will be fine."

"All right, sir. Just thought you should know," I answered. He huffed and sat back behind the steering wheel, impatiently waiting for Jimmy to finish pumping. The seals might hold fine for a few days, or even longer. But he was just tempting fate by not seeing to them.

I closed the hood and walked to the other car. The driver was a woman in her early thirties, by my estimation, with blonde hair done up in a bun. "What can we help you with, ma'am?" I asked.

She flashed me a pretty smile. "Just a fill up, please."

"Yes, ma'am."

I started the pump, then went around to check the engine. The woman drove a Chevy two-door that was only a few years old but had certainly seen better days. The engine was in better shape than the rest of the car, however, and I didn't see any concerns. Jimmy finished up with the surly man and came over to clean the windows of the woman's car. I closed the hood, wiped down the front, and topped off the tank before hanging up the pump.

"That'll be a dollar eighty-two, ma'am," I said, coming around to the driver's side once more.

She smiled again and handed me two dollars. "Thank you. Keep the change."

"Thank you, ma'am. Are you sure?"

She nodded and gave me a little wave before starting her car and pulling away.

Jimmy came up to me, laughing and shaking his head. "What's your secret?"

"Secret?"

"C'mon, Christophe. Don't hold out on me. Me and the other guys don't get tips like that."

I just stared at him blankly for a second. "You don't? I don't know. Just lucky I guess."

Jimmy laughed again. "Okay, okay. I suppose I wouldn't want to tell anybody either."

Confused, I went inside and handed the money over to Rob, who rang the sale into the register. He handed me the eighteen cents and chuckled. "You sure got a way with the ladies."

I had heard this before in my life, but in conjunction with what Laura had said that morning, it got me thinking as I walked back to the garage. I'd always found it easy to make friends. Women, though, had often seemed to want more than just my friendship. And, I'd been happy to oblige them many times in the past.

The past. It always seemed to foul up every relationship. My Hole.

Nearly ten years of my life I couldn't account for. I'd "woken up" in the late twenties and drifted through parts of Montana, the Dakotas, and Nebraska through most of the thirties. In 'forty-two, I came to Cheyenne, Wyoming, and met Laura not long thereafter. She had seemed to accept the Hole and I was thrilled. Our courtship had been short, and not long after the death of Frank's father, her first husband. He had been stationed at Pearl Harbor when the Japanese attacked. Laura was struggling to make ends meet and I was happy to help out. It had been a long time since I'd had any real companionship. We married too soon, at least according to Laura's parents, who refused to ever meet me.

Sometimes I wondered if they'd been right.

I flipped Jimmy the dime out of my tip as I walked past him to the workbench. He was surprised, but, being young, he recovered quickly and caught it with a laugh.

"What's this for?"

"Your part of the tip," I said. "For putting up with the grumpy guy while I helped the lady."

Jimmy smiled. "Thanks!"

"Do you have a girlfriend Jimmy?"

He blushed lightly. "Yeah, I got a girl. Why?"

"Does she get jealous if you talk to other girls?"

"Sometimes. Depends on the girl."

"What do you mean?"

"Well, if I talk to a girl that my girl thinks is pretty, she gets mad. But, if the girl is kinda plain, well, she don't care as much."

I nodded. "I see."

"Your wife don't like you talking with other women?"

I paused before answering. I didn't really want to discuss my personal life with Jimmy, but it was my own fault for bringing it up. "She thinks I'm being unfaithful."

"Are ya?"

Brave kid. Foolish, but that came with the "kid" part. "No," I answered. "I'm not. But I guess I can see how she might think I was." I wondered again who the Sylvie was that Laura heard me call out to in my nightmare. What part did she play in my Hole? Could she have been the cause of it? I tried again to recall the image I had seen, but nothing came.

The knot in my stomach caused me to wince, pulling me

from my reverie. I shook it off and went back to checking over the tools and parts.

The rest of the day contained more of the same. Occasional flurries of pump service, followed by periods of inactivity. I helped out a young man with a bad radiator, and patched a flat tire for another, later in the day. Rob closed the station at 8:30 and we cleaned and prepped for the guys opening up the next morning.

I walked home, enjoying the night air. Hints of autumn were just beginning to intrude on the heat of summer, which made September evenings among my favorite.

I noticed the house was dark, but figured Laura probably had the kids in bed and had turned in early herself. I opened the front door quietly and went to the kitchen to put away my lunch pail and have a glass of milk before heading to bed. After flipping on the light above the sink, I turned to the icebox and something on the kitchen table caught my eye: a sheet of notepaper with Laura's handwriting.

> *Christophe,*
>
> *This is hard for me because you were so kind in my time of need, but I can't go on living with someone who I feel like I don't really know.*
>
> *The kids and I are leaving on the bus this afternoon. We won't be back. Please don't try to follow. This is hard enough on all of us.*
>
> *I truly hope you can find peace in your life someday.*
> *Laura*

Stunned, I read it through twice to be sure I wasn't seeing things. My stomach twisted. Laura and the kids were gone? My mind spun with a thousand thoughts. I knew she'd grown up in Nebraska, likely she'd gone to her parents — in Lincoln? I wasn't sure. Maybe someone at the bus station would remember them and know which one they'd boarded. I folded the note and shoved it in my pants pocket, then I ran to the bedroom to find a jacket.

*Please don't try to follow.*

The image of those words burned like the sun on a blistering August day.

A suitcase was missing from our closet, along with a number of her dresses. Next to the bed, Misty's crib stood empty. Her favorite blanket and teddy bear were gone from their usual place next to her pillow.

How could I not follow?

*This is hard enough on all of us.*

I donned the jacket I'd snatched from the closet and poked my head in Frank's small room next to ours. It was in a neater state than usual with a hastily made bed and little clutter on the floor. Hooks that normally held his baseball mitt and hat were empty.

We didn't own a car since we lived so close to everything we needed. She must have gotten a ride from a friend to the bus station, which was across town. It would be a long walk, but I wasn't about to call anyone at that hour and try to explain why I wanted a ride. After locking the front door, I headed down the street.

Again, my thoughts whirled around our conversation that morning. What had I been reliving in my dreams for me to strike out with enough force to give her a shiner? And who was this Sylvie that Laura said I called out to? I still couldn't bring the memory back that had teased me so briefly. What had happened during all those years I'd lost?

And did I truly want to know?

A familiar stabbing pain in my belly caused me to stop midstride. After collecting myself, I took stock of my surroundings and saw lights across the street. A bar called Manny's, which I had visited from time to time after work, beckoned. I realized I'd neglected having a glass of milk, and that sometimes calmed the demon in my gut. Milk would be in short supply inside, but perhaps some pretzels or nuts would help, I reasoned.

I crossed the street and entered.

Being a weekday evening, few patrons graced the establishment. A young couple occupied a table near the jukebox, which played a Gene Autry song, and a waitress stood next to them, taking their drink order. Two other men sat at the bar, separated by a few stools. Each was engrossed in the glass in front of them. Three ceiling fans lazily circulated cigarette smoke and an earthy smell — likely from the dirt-caked boots of farmhands who frequented the place on weekends. I took a seat at the far end of the bar and Manny himself greeted me.

"Welcome! What can I get ya ... it's Christophe, right?"

I nodded. "I mostly just need something to eat."

Manny produced a bowl of nuts from behind the bar. "You're lookin' pretty low, friend. Need somethin' to wash those down?"

Knowing it would be rude to eat his snacks without ordering something, I nodded again. "Whiskey, please."

Manny quickly poured and set the glass in front of me. "What brings you in tonight, Christophe?"

"Headed to the bus station."

"Oh! Takin' a trip?"

"Not exactly." I popped a handful of nuts in my mouth and pulled Laura's note from my pocket while I chewed. I unfolded it and held it out for Manny to read.

He scanned the message and cringed. "That's some sad business there. You know where she's headed?"

I swallowed and shook my head. "Maybe Lincoln, but I'm not sure. I'm hoping someone at the station will remember her and the kids." I drank the whiskey and sighed.

"I wish you luck," Manny said. "Sounds like she don't want you runnin' after her though."

"I know. But, she's my wife. And they're my kids. Well, the little one anyway. I've got a responsibility."

Manny leaned on the bar close to me. "Seems to me, love should come before responsibility. But, that's just a barkeep talkin'." He poured another whiskey and placed it on the bar. "This one's on the house."

"Thanks," I whispered and he went to check on his other customers.

His comment threw me, as I was sure he'd meant it to. Was I

only going after Laura because I had a responsibility to her and the kids? In truth, I felt responsibility was a good enough reason on its own. But, did I love her? And, possibly more important, were she and the kids better off without me? Had I been too selfish in my desire for a family? Inflicting my Hole and its problems on them really hadn't been fair. Time had refused to heal that particular wound.

I downed the drink and called for another.

I lost track of time after that. Next thing I knew, Manny was leaning in close to me again. "I'm closin' up soon. Can you make it home okay?"

I looked up at him and couldn't focus. "I think so," I said.

Manny looked away and called across the room, "Hey, Jackie! You know where Christophe here lives don't you?"

The waitress, a comfortable looking woman in her late thirties walked to the bar with a rag in her hand. "Yeah. I've seen him walking down Ash Street plenty of times. He's not far from where I live."

"You mind having him walk you home tonight?" Manny asked her.

She smiled at me. "Not at all. That all right with you, Mr. Poinsette?"

I nodded and did my best to stand.

# Margot

*July 9, 1958*

**S**hocked, Margot sat back after bringing Christophe out of his trance.

Had he really said, "Poinsette"?

Margot quickly excused herself and asked one of the nurses to see to Christophe's needs. No doubt he was thirsty and possibly hungry. It had been a long session.

She hurried back to her office and closed the door. Disdaining her awkward chair, she sat on the edge of her desk and mentally kicked herself for not looking into the use of the hospital's tape recorder for her sessions with Christophe. Margot had become accustomed to his slurred speech since his arrival, but now she doubted her ears and desperately wished for a recording to play back.

*That all right with you, Mr. Poinsette?*

Christophe had related his experiences so precisely under the hypnosis that Margot had simply been deep in the flow of note taking — so deep she almost sailed right past the first mention of his surname. When the realization hit, her pen froze in place on the page.

Poinsette was her maiden name.

It had been the only thing she could lay claim to from her missing parents and deceased grandparents. She had treasured it so much over the years that she'd been reluctant to change it when she and Hal had married. Hal, bless his heart, had even been willing to have her keep it but, in the end, Margot had set it aside as an act of letting go of the past and beginning a new and wonderful life.

Yet, as a psychiatrist, she knew people are products of their past. It's not something one can simply forget and hope to live a normal and productive life — just as Christophe had learned during his frustrating, sometimes tortured, existence. One cannot hide forever from oneself. At least not and remain whole.

What did it mean? Poinsette was an unusual name, that much she knew. The likelihood was relatively high that she and Christophe were related, even if distantly. And, of course, another possibility stared her in the face.

*Could Christophe be my father?*

Acknowledging the thought sent her mind reeling again. He was certainly of an age for it to be possible. But, the coincidence of them coming together now? Here? It was beyond belief. More importantly, even if they were related somehow, Margot didn't have a shred of evidence other than Christophe's hypnotically relived memories. Those would never be enough to have him remanded to her care, but they would certainly be enough for Dr. Randolph to order Christophe's further treatment transferred to another doctor due to emotional attachment and conflict of interest.

Dr. Randolph had given her a week to produce some family. She'd actually needed less than a day from all appearances, yet Margot couldn't present her findings now or all her work would be lost.

Suddenly, she was glad for the lack of a recording.

Her left leg had fallen asleep from sitting on the corner of her desk. She hopped down and massaged her hamstring, trying to stimulate the blood flow. Thinking some more, as she rubbed feeling back into her leg, Margot realized she should start with Laura. If she could track down Christophe's estranged wife, then she might be able to gather some concrete evidence of his name and lineage.

The problem was he hadn't been certain where she'd gone, and that had been ten or twelve years in the past. All she could do was try. Margot limped around her desk and picked up the phone's receiver, dialing for the operator.

She spent the better part of an hour trying to find a Laura Poinsette in Lincoln, Nebraska and the surrounding areas with no luck. Margot knew locating her had been a long shot. If Laura had been trying to start a new life, as it had sounded, likely she would have dropped "Poinsette" and gone back to using her previously married name, or her maiden name. But, Christophe hadn't mentioned either of those names in his recollection.

Margot hung up the phone and sat back, frustrated. Even if Laura had kept the name, she could have gone anywhere, or even remarried, in the time that had passed. She would be in her early to mid forties, Margot guessed from the notes she'd taken. The kids would be much older as well. Frank was probably out of the house and on his own, and Misty might be close to starting high school.

Misty!

The thought hit Margot like a lightning bolt. Misty was born in Cheyenne, Wyoming under the surname Poinsette! She checked back through her notebook to be sure. Yes, she confirmed, finding the passage; Christophe had said he and Laura had met and married after he'd arrived in Cheyenne. Laura's first husband had been killed at Pearl Harbor, which had been in December of 1941. Christophe mentioned Laura's parents being upset at the short amount of time before she'd married him so, Margot surmised, they had probably tied the knot in '42 or '43, and Misty had been born some time after that.

With renewed energy, Margot picked up the telephone again. After a few minutes, she reached St. Joseph Hospital in Cheyenne and asked for their records department.

"This is Dianne, how can I help you?"

"Hello, Dianne, this is Dr. Margot Braun with the Colorado State Hospital in Pueblo, and I'm looking for the records, preferably a birth certificate, of a Misty Poinsette that would have been born in the summer of 1943 or '44."

"You don't have the specific date?"

"I'm sorry, I don't," Margot said. "Her father, Christophe Poinsette, is here in our facility, and I'm trying to locate either

Misty, or her mother."

"All right. Let me see what I can find. It may take some time to sort out. Can I confirm the spellings and get a number to reach you?"

Margot gave her the information and hung up, anticipation twisting her belly. With nothing to do but wait, she glanced at the clock and realized it was nearly time to make her afternoon rounds. She also noted she hadn't had anything to eat since early that morning.

Pushing away from the desk, Margot headed to the kitchens for a snack and then to check on her other patients.

As a new hire, beginning at the bottom of the totem pole, she had been assigned the most irredeemable cases — those with no hope of cure or change. Several had been lobotomized, as had been customary for a time with cases that were typically violent and hadn't responded well to other treatments. Margot often wondered what went on in those lost minds. How did they view the world?

One patient, who was a favorite of hers, was an elderly woman named Edna. Edna didn't speak, or even appear to interact with the world at first glance. She simply sat, silent and unmoving, in her wheelchair, throughout the day — unless she was moved away from a window. Then, her features would sour and she would emit a low moan of distress. Put her back in front of the window, and it was as if nothing had happened. Margot sometimes sat next to Edna, studying her face and eyes as she stared blankly through the glass. What sorts of thoughts wandered through her broken mind? Margot thought of Edna as a flower — needing the light of day to bloom and survive. Once the sun had set, Edna could be wheeled back to her room without fuss or reaction. Cases like Edna's fascinated Margot and sometimes she fantasized about having telepathic powers, like those in the pulp science fiction stories, so she could look inside the thoughts of her charges. Did they still think and feel like the rest of us? Or were their minds completely alien without the ability to communicate or be understood?

The complexity of the human brain was a constant marvel for Margot. Christophe's case was certainly no exception. His memory was evidently still intact, but somehow hidden from his conscious thoughts by a mechanism Margot didn't begin to understand. Had something so horrific happened in his past that the only method available to his mind to cope was to shut years of his life away forever? Or had he suffered some external injury that had damaged his brain, making the normal process of memory and recall impossible? Maybe it was a combination of the two, or something else entirely she hadn't considered.

Margot needed more information.

She completed her rounds and returned to her office, preparing to leave for the day. After she had packed up her notebook and purse, the phone rang. Hope sparked in her chest as she lifted the receiver. "Hello?"

"Dr. Braun, I have Dianne from St. Joseph Hospital on the line for you."

"Yes, put her through, please."

After a couple of clicks, Margot heard, "Dr. Braun?"

"Yes, Dianne?"

"Hello, yes. I wanted to let you know I did find a record of birth for Misty. Date of birth was July 30, 1944. Would you like me to mail a copy to your office?"

Elation filled Margot. Finally, she was getting somewhere! "That would be excellent, but would you mind reading me some of the information? I'm looking for Laura's — the mother's — maiden name, and hometown if you have it."

"The mother is listed as Laura Jeane Haupner. And yes, we do have a hometown: Cortland, Nebraska."

Margot hastily scribbled in her notebook. "Thank you so much." She gave Dianne the hospital's address to send the copy and hung up with a smile on her face.

By the time she got home, Margot's thoughts had turned back to Christophe's name and the possible repercussions to her own life. Could he really be her father? If so, what had happened to her mother?

Hal had arrived at the house just a few minutes earlier and the two of them set about preparing dinner together in the kitchen. Margot's mind fretted over the puzzle of her missing parents and she silently went through the motions of chopping vegetables while Hal grilled Salisbury steaks on an iron skillet. Once the food was cooked, they sat together at the table.

"All right," Hal said. "Spill it."

Startled, Margot looked up at him. "What?"

"Your head's buzzin' so fast smoke's comin' out your ears.

Tell me. What's got you all tied up in knots?"

Margot sighed, then chuckled, realizing Hal was right. She forced herself to relax and cut a bite of steak. "I had a rather interesting day. I found out Christophe had a wife, and a daughter who's about fourteen years old now."

"That's good. Did he get his memory back then?"

"No. I learned this all through hypnosis. But I got confirmation of it just before I came home. The hospital in Cheyenne where his daughter was born called me back. They had her birth records."

"Terrific," Hal said as he chewed. "So, now you can get a hold of his family, right?"

"It's not that simple, unfortunately. His wife left him some time in '46. I got the feeling they haven't seen each other since."

"Hm. What's your next move then?"

"I have the wife's name and the town where she grew up. I guess I'll start there. See if her parents or some other family are still around."

"Uh huh," he said, looking up at her. Then he pointed his fork in her direction. "There's something else. I see it in your eyes. Or is it doctor-patient stuff you can't talk about?"

Margot's gaze dropped to her plate. "No, it's not that. I found out his last name. It's Poinsette."

Hal stared for a second, then set his fork down. "Isn't that your ... now, wait a minute. You don't think you're related to this guy, do you?"

"I don't know. That's the problem."

"Look. I know it's not a common name, but what are the chances?"

She raised her eyes again and met his. "I realize that. But, what if he is?"

"Isn't there some way you can find out? Contact the orphanage you were in, or something?"

Margot sighed and sat back. "I tried that years ago. I was in college and got especially curious about my birth family. They'd had a big fire at the orphanage about three years before and everything was lost. All the records were burned. I even went back to the town where my grandparents had lived. But it had been almost twenty years and no one could tell me anything about them. After checking some records in the courthouse there, I found out they were French immigrants and bought their farm around 1885, but there was nothing else."

"And your foster parents didn't have any information either?"

"No. Nothing beyond what I already knew. My grandmother didn't live long after grandpa died and she sold the farm. I'm not even sure where she was buried."

They finished their meal in silence. Hal got up to clear the dishes, putting them in the sink for washing. He turned to her then and asked, "You said you know where his wife grew up?"

Margot joined him in their small kitchen and began to fill the sink with water. "Yes. It's in Nebraska. Cortland, I think."

Hal nodded. "Been through there once. Small town, not far from Lincoln." He moved to her right and grabbed a hand towel.

"Think you'll be able to handle business over the telephone? Or you plannin' on headin' out there?"

She added some soap to the water. "I hadn't thought about going, no. I sure hope it doesn't come to that. I won't have time."

"What do you mean?"

"Dr. Randolph only gave me a week to find Christophe's family before he turns the case over to another doctor."

"Well, sounds like you found some family. Or almost at least. What's the problem?"

Margot handed him a clean, wet plate. "I haven't told him what I found out today. He's skeptical about Christophe's memory loss and the hypnosis I've been doing. If he found out about our common last name, he'd likely pull me off the case immediately. He already thinks I'm too emotionally involved."

"Are you?" he asked while drying the plate.

"Of course I am! How could I not be? But I have to help him, Hal. I need to know."

"What about Christophe? Does he need to know?"

Margot paused, surprised at the question. "Yes. I believe it's the only way he can ever heal."

After they'd finished the dishes, Margot decided to make some telephone calls. The evening was still young, and she thought it might be a better time to reach Laura, or her folks, rather than trying when she got back to the office in the morning. Plus, waiting promised to drive her crazy. A few minutes later, the local operator made the connection.

"Cortland switchboard, how may I direct your call?"

"Hello, yes, I don't have a number, but I'm looking for anyone with the last name of Haupner, who lives there in Cortland."

"I have a George and Myrna Haupner."

"Perfect," Margot said.

"Connecting, one moment."

The line went quiet for a split second, then began ringing.

"Hello?" the voice of an elderly woman answered.

"Hello, Mrs. Haupner?"

"Yes, who is this?"

"My name is Dr. Margot Braun, from Pueblo, Colorado, and I'm trying to locate someone. Do you, by chance, have a daughter named Laura?"

Silence answered Margot for several heartbeats. Then Mrs. Haupner said, "We do."

*Oh! Thank goodness!*

"I'm sorry, doctor," Mrs. Haupner continued. "What is this about? Has she been hurt?"

"No, no," Margot said. "I'm sorry if I've frightened you Mrs. Haupner. I'm just trying to locate Laura. It's in regard to your granddaughter Misty's father." Margot braced herself, knowing Christophe's relations with Laura's parents hadn't been good.

"Misty's father?" Margot heard a muffled voice in the background, then Mrs. Haupner said, "I don't know, someone asking about Misty's father."

"Mrs. Haupner, I really need to get in touch with Laura. Can you tell me where she is, or give me a telephone number?" Margot asked, feeling she was losing control of the conversation.

She heard some shuffling on the other end of the line, then a gruff male voice said, "Hello? Who is this?"

Frustrated, Margot did her best to calm her nerves. "I'm Dr. Margot Braun, Mr. Haupner, and I'm trying to locate your daughter, Laura."

"What's this about Misty's father? That monster caused Laura enough trouble and we've all been trying to forget him —"

"Mr. Haupner, please," Margot interrupted. "I understand you're upset, but it's very important that I speak to Laura. Christophe, Misty's father, has been injured and —"

"Injured? Good!" Margot heard the fury in his voice. "He's lucky to still be breathing after what he did to my little girl! If I'd been younger ... well, let's just say it's a good thing he didn't come looking for Laura years ago."

In the background, Margot caught Mrs. Haupner's voice, "George, calm down."

"Mr. Haupner," Margot began. "I can understand your anger. I know their relationship didn't end well, but please hear me out. There will come a time when Misty will want to know about her father — for better or worse. As someone who was abandoned by her parents, I'm asking you please, don't deny Misty the opportunity to decide for herself about Christophe."

Mr. Haupner sighed heavily. "Dr. Braun, do you have children? Grandchildren?"

Margot cringed inside. "No."

"Then let me just say, if you did, you would not be talking to me right now. That man beat my daughter. I saw the effects of it with my own eyes. I think I can judge what's best for her and my granddaughter. They don't need to have anything more to do with him. Goodbye, Dr. Braun."

The line clicked dead and Margot set the receiver back in its cradle, her hand shaking.

If she'd been honest with herself, Margot realized the Haupners' reaction was one she should have expected, but her excitement had overridden caution and good sense. Time also pressed her. The need to produce a verifiable family member to direct Christophe's care weighed heavily on her mind. If she couldn't do that, he would officially become a ward of the State, and Dr. Randolph could prescribe whatever treatment he saw fit, regardless of Margot's belief that she might be related to Christophe somehow. Dr. Randolph would see it as nothing more than feminine weakness — maternal emotional attachment.

Margot discovered she was weeping. Tears slid from her cheek into her lap, darkening random spots in the plain dress she wore. The stains spread slowly through the fabric, reminding her of ink blot cards. What did these images represent to her? Emotional attachment. How could anyone not become emotional about patients under their care? She had to be truthful though, and admit this case, this patient, was something far beyond the boundaries of normal. Christophe's past likely held secrets vital to not only his mental wellbeing, but possibly her own as well.

She felt a strong hand on her shoulder and looked up through watery eyes at Hal's rugged face. He gave her a small smile as she took his hand in her own.

"I take it the conversation didn't go quite as you'd hoped," he said gently.

Margot chuckled and wiped her remaining tears away with her other hand. "That would be an understatement."

"So, what's the plan?"

She sighed and smiled back at him. Hal was a mechanic, through and through. Much like a doctor, she realized, he diagnosed problems and sought a cure. In a sense, Dr. Randolph was right. She needed to gain some detachment in order to get a better view of her dilemma. "I'm not sure yet," she answered finally. "They knew him. That much was clear. And just as clear, they want nothing more to do with him. Somehow, I have to find Laura. I feel like she would be more sympathetic — for Misty's benefit if nothing else."

They moved to the sofa and sat together. "This Laura is his ex-wife?" Hal asked.

Margot nodded. "Her parents still live in Cortland. That's who I talked to. But they wouldn't tell me where Laura is."

The two sat quietly, Hal with his arm protectively around her shoulder. Margot puzzled through her options. If Laura had taken her maiden name again, she probably wouldn't be hard to find, if only Margot knew what city to look in. She thought back through the conversation, but couldn't pick out any clues.

"I've got some buddies in Nebraska I've been meaning to go see," Hal announced. "Think I might ask for a few days off from work and take me a trip."

Margot turned her head, seeing a mischievous look in his eyes. "I can't ask you to do that."

"Ask me to do what? All I said was I wanted to go visit some friends of mine."

"You scamp. You know what I'm talking about."

"The way I see it, you need to be in two places at once. Maybe this is a way you can."

"I don't know," Margot said.

"I suppose I could go to the hospital and put the whammy on Christophe while you go to Nebraska …"

She leaned back and punched him in the shoulder. "Don't make fun!" she said, laughing. "All right. I'll write down what information I have. But if you can't get the time off, then just forget it. I'll think of something."

"Never a doubt in my mind but you would," Hal whispered and leaned in for a kiss.

# Margot

## *July 10, 1958*

Margot arrived at the hospital in the morning with a new sense of determination. She knew the work she'd done already with Christophe was on the right track, but she needed to be more scientific in her approach. After performing her usual rounds, she sat in her office with a set of texts on memory and hypnosis.

The practice and technique of hypnotism had seen increased attention since the early fifties and had become an accepted practice and treatment. Pope Pius XII had even approved the use of hypnosis for healthcare professionals two years earlier. Margot felt it to be a sound method to access the subconscious and her successes with Christophe thus far seemed to validate her belief. Her biggest concern was Christophe's inability to recall anything from the sessions afterward. She feared something was lacking in her application or execution of the procedure.

She also struggled with reconciling her results in Christophe's case with some of the teachings she'd held dear during her education. Psychology was roughly divided into two camps: Freud and Jung. Though Jung had been a student and colleague of Freud's, the two had parted ways, largely as a result of differences in their views of the unconscious mind. In very general terms, Freud felt the unconscious was merely a dumping ground for unwanted thoughts and desires, and largely sexual in nature. Jung believed the unconscious played a more active role in human development and personality. Margot held to many of Jung's ideas yet, Christophe's mind appeared to be treating his memories as refuse and shunting them off to his unconscious, more along the lines of a Freudian model. Reality, she knew, was probably somewhere in the middle, but finding that middle ground had so far proved difficult at best.

In her research, Margot stumbled across a reference to Jung and his use of art in some of his therapies. She remembered much about the practice from her days at the university and decided that coming at the problem from a different angle might shed some more light in the dark areas of Christophe's mind. A number of patients at the hospital had responded favorably to such activities in the past.

She went to one of the storerooms and found a drawing tablet, some charcoal, and a handful of crayons. After talking with an intern about bringing a tape recorder to Christophe's room, Margot made her way there with the art supplies.

He had just finished his lunch and a nurse was clearing the dishes. Christophe's face brightened and he gave Margot his lopsided smile. "Hello, Dr. Braun. Good to ssssee you."

"And you. How are you feeling today?"

"Fine. Nursssse Blanche gave me a treat," he said with a chuckle.

Margot looked at the nurse and saw her cheeks color. "I just put a little cinnamon in his applesauce," she said with a shy smile.

"Well, I'm sure there's no harm in that," Margot replied. "Thank you, Nurse."

Nurse Blanche smiled again. "You're welcome, Dr. Braun." She left with her tray and closed the door.

"Ahh you going to make me ssspill more sssecretss today?"

It was Margot's turn to chuckle. "No. I thought we'd try something different today." She put the drawing pad in his lap and set the charcoal and crayons on the table next to the bed.

"I'm no ahtissst."

"You don't have to be an artist. It's more about bringing feelings to the paper. Just pick a color that seems right and let your mind wander and your hand do what it will."

"Okay. I'll try."

There was a knock at the door and the intern Margot had spoken to earlier entered with one of the hospital's bulky tape recorders. They spent the next several minutes setting it up and making sure it worked properly. The tape tended to bind up if the tension wasn't just right.

Margot thanked him and closed the door once more, turning back to Christophe. He had taken a crayon and applied it to the paper while Margot had fussed with the recorder. "How is it going?" she asked him.

Christophe set the crayon aside. "I don't think thisss iss helping."

He turned the pad toward her and Margot's hand involuntarily went to her mouth.

Christophe had covered almost the entire page in solid red.

She took the pad from him and sat down. "Why did you do this?"

"I don't know. You told me to pick a colah and let my mind wandah. All I sssaw wasss red."

Margot arrived home that evening still somewhat disturbed by Christophe's drawing. She found herself forced to reconsider Dr. Randolph's assertion that Christophe had been untruthful about his condition. Was he just playing a game? The more she thought about it, though, the more she rejected the notion. Christophe's level of sincerity when he spoke with her was something she didn't believe could be faked on a consistent basis. A talented actor could pull it off for a session or two, maybe, but slips would happen. Mistakes would be made. She had seen none of that in the time she'd spent with him.

On her way to the kitchen, she saw a note on the dining table.

*Got the time off and decided to head out. I'll phone you later. Don't have too much fun without me!*

*— Hal*

Margot smiled. *Same to you, Mister!* she chuckled.

# Margot

*July 11, 1958*

**S**he tossed and turned most of the night and woke bleary-eyed and tired. Fleeting dreams of her childhood and her grandparents haunted her during the time she did sleep. Margot kept a small notebook beside the bed, having always been interested in dreams, but the memories faded too quickly to jot down anything meaningful.

In all honesty, it wasn't difficult to determine the reason for her restlessness. The desire to know if Christophe was her father burned brightly inside her. The possibility to discover, after all these years, what had become of her parents filled her thoughts to distraction. Margot had carefully bundled up her feelings of family and her past long ago and set them aside. The intensity those feelings held on reexamination surprised her. The need for a sense of belonging was stronger than she'd ever realized or acknowledged.

Hal had called from a payphone, just before she'd gone to bed, and told her he'd made it to some small town outside of Hastings, Nebraska, and was spending the night with a friend.

He promised he would call again once he had any information on Laura.

Margot smiled at the thought of him as she drove to work after a hurried breakfast. She wondered, not for the first time, at their chance first meeting and if there had been some outside guiding force involved. Fate, karma, God — as a woman of science she often had little patience for such notions, but lately she had been confronted with a number of incidents that seemed to beg for explanations beyond her science.

Jung had postulated a shared level of consciousness among all people. He used it to explain the wealth of similarities in basic beliefs and stories among the many religions of the world. Margot wondered if perhaps something like Jung's collective consciousness acted as some form of guide, driving people's belief in fate, or divine providence. Such thoughts, of course, were blasphemy to the tenets of the church she had grown up with, but she had been looking for answers to questions outside her religious beliefs since an early age.

After arriving at the hospital, Margot collected the few notes in her mail slot, then stopped in the small staff break room to pour herself a cup of coffee. Taking a sip, she turned to see Nurse Blanche walking in the doorway.

"Dr. Braun! I'm glad you're here. Christophe was asking for you at breakfast."

"Thank you, Blanche. I'll go see him right away."

Margot took her coffee and stopped by her office just long enough to drop off her purse and make sure she had nothing urgent to attend to in her notes. She grabbed her notebook and headed to Christophe's room.

He looked up when she entered, but didn't give her his usual smile. She closed the door and sat in her usual spot next to the bed.

"Nurse Blanche said you wanted to see me. Is something wrong?"

Christophe sighed. "I don't know. I had sssome nightmaresss."

Margot reached over and turned on the recorder, setting the microphone near the edge of the table, then opened her notebook. "Can you tell me about them?"

"I don't remembah mussch. Jussst bad feelingsss. And blood. Lotsss of blood."

Margot noted his speech was more slurred than it had been the past few days. He truly seemed upset. "Try to relax. We'll get this figured out. It may be connected with your drawing yesterday. Do you think it was your blood? Or someone else's?"

He thought briefly. "Ssssomeone elssse I think. What doesss it mean?"

"Christophe, my first impression is I think your memories are trying to return. Some of them have been blocked for so long, I doubt the process is going to be easy."

"But. All the blood …" He trailed off, then his right eye grew wide. "Do you think I hurt ssssomeone?"

Margot put a hand on his arm. "I don't know. I don't believe the person you are now would ever harm anyone intentionally. Maybe there was a terrible accident that your mind has tried to forget."

"The perssssson I am now," he repeated. "Maybe I wanted to forget that I was ssssomeone elssse."

Margot sighed. "It's possible. But, let's not think negative. What we need to do is find the root of the blockage. What was it that caused your brain to want to turn away from itself and those memories? I think we need to try to explore that time you've referred to as your 'Hole' during the hypnosis we've done so far."

"Have I sssaid when that wassss?"

She nodded. "You gave me a better idea at least during our last session. If you're feeling up to it, we can try again as soon as I've made my regular rounds."

"I think I'd like that. It'ssss time to put an end to thissss."

"All right," she said with a pat on his arm. "I'll be back a little later."

Margot left and went to catch up on her morning routine. Her deadline from Dr. Randolph loomed large in her mind. She only had another four or five days, at best, to produce some concrete results, but she also couldn't neglect her other patients and duties.

Another thing troubling her was deciding on what time period to direct Christophe's thoughts to for their next session. Margot had been born in 1922, which was during the span he had indicated for his Hole, and she desperately wanted to find the answers to her own questions in addition to determining the cause of his problem. But, was it fair to zero in on that point in time? Was she being too self-serving in choosing to start there?

She knew what Dr. Randolph's response would be. And she felt doubly uncomfortable that part of her agreed with him.

She finished dispensing medications then stopped by the kitchens for a cup of juice and some crackers in case Christophe wanted a snack. As she left, moving into the stark hallway, she saw Nurse Blanche pushing a cart of bed linens. Margot, knowing she would be skating on thin ice with Dr. Randolph from this point forward, made a decision to try to recruit some aid to her cause. Taking care not to spill the juice, she quickened her pace to catch up with Blanche.

"Excuse me, Nurse, do you have a minute?"

Blanche stopped the cart and looked up at Margot. "Of course, Doctor. What is it?"

The young woman was in her early twenties with dark hair done up in a traditional bun. Margot searched her hazel eyes and said, "Do you mind if I call you Blanche?" The nurse shook her head. "I think we get carried away with being too formal around here sometimes."

Blanche smiled. "It does get a bit stuffy sometimes, Dr. Braun."

"Please, call me Margot. I wanted to ask you something."

"Yes?"

"What do you think of Christophe?"

Margot was surprised to note Blanche's cheeks color slightly. "He's a sweet man. I really feel sorry for him."

"Why's that?"

"Well, it doesn't seem right for him to be ... in a place like this. I mean, he's smart, and funny, and just not …"

"Insane?" Margot finished for her.

Blanche's eyes widened. "I don't mean —"

"No, no. It's okay. I completely agree with you. He doesn't belong in this type of facility, but right now, he doesn't have anywhere else to go. I'm trying to fix that, but I think I'm going to need some assistance. Do you think you could help me out?"

"Of course, Doc — I mean, Margot," she said, smiling at her mistake.

"Good," Margot replied with a smile of her own. "I'm going to need two things. I will probably be spending a lot of time with Christophe over the next few days. Any help I can get in keeping an eye on my other patients would be appreciated."

Blanche nodded. "Certainly."

Margot set the cup and crackers down on Blanche's cart and wrote in her notebook. "Here's my telephone number at home. If you are working a shift when I'm not here and notice anything unusual — anything at all — will you please call me?" She tore off the paper and handed it to Blanche.

The nurse pocketed the number and nodded again. "I'd be happy to."

Margot smiled again. "Thank you. I won't keep you any longer."

Blanche sighed. "I appreciate the distraction from changing beds," she said leaning into the cart once Margot had retrieved her juice and snack.

Feeling better, Margot watched the young nurse make her

way down the hall, then turned and focused her thoughts on Christophe. Clinically, the only approach that made sense was to start at the beginning of his lost time and work their way through. Her own desires were secondary to finding the cause of Christophe's neurosis. If she were fortunate, maybe she'd find her own answers along the way.

Entering his room, she closed the door, then sat and offered him the drink and food. She checked the recorder, making sure everything was still in order while he nibbled and drank.

After he finished, she took the empty plate and cup and took a deep breath. "All right. Clear your mind and think back to the time around the start of World War I ..."

# Christophe

## *July 17, 1918*

I had heard it said a soldier's life is one of utter boredom and monotony, sprinkled with flashes of sheer terror.

I knew well the boredom and monotony.

After finishing my turn at patrol of the camp perimeter, I collapsed in the two-man tent I shared with Tony Amato, my uniform soaked with sweat. Thankfully, Tony was elsewhere as I could barely stand my own stink, never mind someone else's. The tent offered little relief from the afternoon heat, but it did shade my eyes from the bright sun.

I lay, unmoving, for a time, all my gear still strapped uncomfortably around my body. I had gone to war with lofty dreams of liberating my parents' homeland from evil oppressors. Remembered tales, told by my mother when I was a boy, of sprawling vineyards and idyllic pastoral scenes had filled my thoughts while my compatriots and I had been on the ship ferrying us across the Atlantic. Those images had been quickly dashed away by the realities of war. The scenery I saw most often was the back of the fellow in front of me as we marched for days on end across the French countryside after our landing on the northern coast. The quaint villas and chateaus I'd imagined were replaced by the bombed ruins of village after village on our trek east. I soon lost track of the days as they blended seamlessly together, each one a nearly perfect replica of the one before.

The toe of a boot impacted my leg and I realized I must have dozed off.

"Christophe, Sarge is lookin' for you," I heard Tony's voice through my mental haze.

I groaned and rolled over, my equipment poking me to wakefulness. "Why?"

Tony laughed. "You know better'n to ask that. I don't know. He's by the mess tent. You better hurry."

I levered myself up and suddenly understood why my father made so much noise when he got out of bed in the mornings. I was only twenty years old. I shouldn't be sounding like him already.

"Mess tent?" I asked.

Tony nodded. "And you better double-time, it took me a while to find you."

Briefly I wondered where Tony had thought to look for me before deciding to try our tent, but it wasn't important. Tony wasn't the sharpest tack in the box, but he'd been a good tentmate. He didn't snore too loud and had never taken anything without asking first. The same couldn't be said for a lot of the other fellows.

I made a quick check of my gear and grabbed my rifle before

jogging the hundred yards or more to the mess tent.

We were billeted two or three miles southeast of Chateau Thierry — at least that was my understanding, I hadn't actually seen the place yet. We had come back west from Verdun a few days before to support the Sixth. Word had it something big was in the works.

I spotted Sergeant Hayes and ran to him, stopping sharply and kicking up a small cloud of dust.

"Took yer sweet time gettin' here, Private," he said in a gruff voice, roughened from years of yelling at the top of his considerable lungs.

Flustered, I wasn't sure how to respond. "Yes, Sergeant! I mean, no, Sergeant. I mean, Private Amato said you wanted to see me."

"You speak French don't you, Poinsette?" He always said my name to rhyme with "coin" instead of the proper French pronunciation. It never seemed important to correct him.

"My parents are French and I learned it as a boy, but it's been a while, sir."

"I didn't ask for your family history, Private! Yes, or no?"

"Yes, Sergeant!"

"Follow me."

He turned and strode smartly in the direction of the command tents. I followed closely, knowing anything else would result in a tongue lashing at the very least, but I was perplexed as to why the Sergeant cared if I spoke French.

My ears focused momentarily on the ever-present sounds

of artillery shells exploding in the distance. Those same sounds, that I now mostly ignored, had been the cause of many sleepless nights for the first month or more of my time in France. We had drilled endlessly in training Stateside for what we would encounter overseas, but they couldn't accurately recreate the feelings and emotions of actually being on the battlefield. That was something we'd just had to overcome on our own.

We arrived at one of the officers' tents and Sergeant Hayes pulled the canvas flap aside. The two of us entered together and saluted. I couldn't see right away just who we were saluting, but it was a safe bet we needed to.

"At ease," a smooth voice said.

I dropped my arm and surveyed the tent as my eyes adjusted to the relative dark inside. What little breeze there was outside was blocked by the thick canvas, creating a sauna-like atmosphere. The strong smell of unwashed bodies mixed with tobacco of various types. I recognized Major Yates, a balding man in his late thirties or early forties of average height. Next to him stood a taller man wearing a dusty, dark top, with the first few buttons undone, and a pair of bright red pants trimmed with a wide, black strip of fabric down the side of each leg. A pair of aviator's goggles sat perched on top of his head.

Major Yates looked up from a paper he'd been reading and met my eyes. I stiffened and concentrated on a piece of canvas past his left ear. Yates then glanced to Sergeant Hayes. "I assume this is the young man you spoke of, Sergeant?"

"Yes, sir!"

"Very good, thank you, Sergeant, that will be all."

Hayes saluted again and left the tent. Major Yates turned his attention to me once more. "Private, I'm in a bit of a pickle and I'm hoping you can help."

"Of course, sir. What exactly did you need help with, sir?"

"I've been charged with getting more information about the disposition of the Jerries' forces north of the Marne, but given few resources to do so. I've managed to secure a plane from the Brits, and now, a pilot." Yates gestured to his right. "This is Captain Thibideaux. He has volunteered to fly the mission, but his observer was wounded on their last flight and is in hospital."

I nodded slowly. "I'm sorry, sir, but I'm still unsure what you need of me."

"Captain Thibideaux speaks very little English. Sergeant Hayes was under the impression that you speak French, yes?"

"Yes, sir. So, you need me to translate for you?"

Yates chuckled. "No, Son. I speak enough French to get by. I need you to go with him and be his observer."

*His observer!* My heart raced. I'd had some observer training and performed some basic ground-based tasks in Verdun, but now I was going to fly?!

"Private? Are you all right?" the Major asked.

Startled, I stammered back, "Y-yes, sir! Sorry, sir!"

Major Yates smiled and handed me a leather-bound journal. "Very good. Follow the Captain's instructions to the letter and report back to me once you've returned. You can leave your rifle here. There won't be room for it on the airplane."

I leaned my weapon against the table and saluted. "Yes, sir!"

Yates pointed to the tent flap and said to Thibideaux, "*Bon chance.*"

The Captain gave Yates a small smile. "*Merci.*"

I followed the pilot outside and he led me away from our camp at a brisk pace. Afternoon had turned to evening and the heat was slowly beginning to dissipate. The sun wouldn't fully set for a few more hours, but I was sure the Captain would want to get airborne as soon as possible.

As we walked across a field of dry grass, trodden flat from countless footfalls, I marveled at this turn of events. One of my dreams had been to work on machinery, airplanes in particular, and I'd hoped my conscription in the army would give me a chance to do that. Thus far, my dreams had been flattened by the drudgery of a soldier's life, much like the ground we strode upon. Now, perhaps, I'd have an opportunity to grasp a bit of the dream. Sylvie would be so proud!

I looked up and saw it. A two-seat bi-wing with a mottled paint job which did a poor job of covering up numerous repairs and patches. Two of the wing struts were tightly wrapped with cloth and coated in resin, doubtless in an attempt to mend a crack or other weak spot. An attendant stood by the engine, rubbing down the four-bladed propeller.

Captain Thibideaux stopped once he saw the plane. "*Merde,*" was his only comment.

Being as this was the first airplane I'd seen up close, the little boy in me wanted to passionately disagree. It was a marvelous machine! The mechanic in me though, had to support the Captain's statement. The plane did bare similarities to a steaming pile of excrement.

Up close, it didn't get any better.

The fuselage was marred by numerous holes and pockmarks — some patched, some not. Thibideaux slowly walked around the plane, inspecting each flaw. Once he reached the nose, he spoke rapidly in French to the attendant, who I realized was little more than a boy. I struggled to keep up with the conversation; it had been a long time since I'd sat at our kitchen table and spoken French with my parents.

Leaving the two to talk, I stepped closer to the motor and looked it over. No cowling covered it, whether by design or accident I didn't know. Old and new oil caked the outside, making it difficult to identify individual parts. Most engines were built on the same principles: they had cylinders, with pistons inside attached to rods which moved them up and down in synchronized fashion. I noticed a rag hooked around a wing strut next to me. Without thinking, I picked it up and began to wipe off the cylinder heads.

"*Attendez! Tu est mécanicien?*" Captain Thibideaux said and it took me a moment to realize he was talking to me.

"I'm sorry! *Eh, pardon. Oui, en peu, Capitaine.*" I stammered.

"*C'est vrai? Tres bien! Pouvez-vous fixer?*" He wanted to know if I could fix it.

"*Je ne sais pas. Quel est le problème?*" I asked.

Thibideaux threw up his hands in disgust, then spoke rapid-fire, gesturing vehemently at the engine.

"Slow down, please. Ah, shoot. *Ralentir, s'il vous plaît.*"

The Captain stopped ranting, then looked at me and laughed. I felt heat in my cheeks in spite of the warm temperature. He stuck his hand out and said, "*Pardon. Je m'appelé Henri.*"

Once I figured out that he wasn't upset with me, I smiled and shook his hand. "Christophe."

"*Très bien. Enchanté.*" He then did his best to explain what was wrong with the motor. Between his description and the visual evidence everywhere, it was clear the plane had an oil leak.

I asked if any tools were available and climbed up onto the fuselage for a better look. Captain Thibideaux consulted briefly with the young attendant, who then ran back toward the encampment. The right side of the beast was significantly dirtier than the left, so I concentrated my search there, cleaning as I went. A few minutes and several filthy rags later, the boy returned with a handful of wrenches. I tightened everything I could see, working quickly, knowing we were running out of daylight even in the height of summer.

I sat up and surveyed my work. Without understanding more about the particulars of the engine, I'd done all I could. I shrugged and told the Captain as much. He beckoned me down and explained how to start it from the propeller. I took my position as he climbed in the cockpit and donned his cap and goggles. He gave me a thumbs up and I cranked the prop. It sputtered twice, then caught on the third try.

I stepped back as he throttled up. The motor's timing

sounded slightly off to me, but I didn't think it would affect its performance overmuch. Much more concerning was the possibility of a major leak. Fortunately, I couldn't see any signs of new oil from where I stood.

Evidently satisfied, Captain Thibideaux motioned for me to climb aboard. I hesitated only briefly before stepping onto the wing and hauling myself into the second seat. I found a leather flight cap and goggles inside and put them on. The cap was just a little big, but the chin strap held it firm. Much better than it being too small. The goggles made it difficult to see, but no more so than a gas mask. I looked up and saw Henri's head looking back at me and I stuck my thumb up to let him know I was ready, even though my legs and arms felt like jelly.

He smiled and turned his attention forward. The engine revved and the plane started to move. I found myself holding my breath as we bumped over the field, then suddenly, everything was smooth. I turned my head and saw the ground falling away. We were airborne!

I leaned over just a bit and located the camp. It looked much more orderly from the air than it seemed on the ground. We circled once to gain altitude, then headed north I deduced once I'd oriented myself by the setting sun to my left.

Trying to calm the butterflies in my stomach, I pulled out the journal Major Yates had given me. In a pocket inside, I found three pencils and a drawing compass for creating circles and measuring distances. I turned to a blank page and did my best to sketch out the camp and the Marne river as we passed over it. The area north of the Marne was a patchwork of forest and farmland. Below, to my left, I spotted what must have been the town of Chateau Thierry and marked its location on my drawing.

Looking down to the right, I saw a handful of tiny villages and more farms and groves of trees. Occasionally, puffs of smoke materialized from different places on the ground. Before long I made the connection that these were German artillery shells being fired on the Allied forces. The constant pops and booms I heard and had learned to ignore on the ground were drowned out by the airplane's motor. Reducing the activity to simple smoky puffs made it seem almost peaceful somehow. Less threatening.

Henri banked slightly to the left — port, I mentally corrected myself — and noted somewhat less of the forest had been cleared for farming. I continued to draw, to the best of my meager artistic abilities, and mark a point wherever I saw the telltale smoke from heavy gun fire. Captain Thibideaux's portside turn smoothly transitioned into a slow starboard one. He was making a large circle of the land north of the Marne and I continued to scribble furiously. Without knowledge of the local landmarks, it was nearly impossible for me to estimate distances, and I only hoped that the work I was doing would be of some benefit to Major Yates and the other officers.

A cloud of smoke appeared to my right, almost level with the plane, accompanied by a resounding crack.

"*Tenez!*" Henri shouted ahead of me. I obeyed and held tight to the thick wood trim of my cockpit.

The plane dipped sharply to port and the world tilted sickeningly. I shut my eyes which eased my vertigo, but only a little. The engine strained as Henri pushed the throttle for more speed. I caught the journal with my left hand, barely before it slid off my lap. The pencil and compass clattered to the floor by my feet. After shoving the journal under my thigh, I resumed my firm grip on the rail.

"*Deux heures!*"

Two o'clock. I opened my eyes and searched in that direction. Out of the setting sun I saw it. A fighter plane with a distinct tri-wing silhouette. German! I spared a glance behind me to the empty mounting bracket where a machine gun had once been placed. It had been removed some time in the past, no doubt to put it to better use on a plane that wasn't falling apart. I didn't know if Henri had shouted to me only in warning or if he'd forgotten our plane was unarmed.

We rolled back to starboard and I lost sight of the German fighter. Another reverberating boom assaulted my ears, somewhere behind us I thought, but couldn't be sure. Soon after, I heard the rapid pops of impacting bullets. Bits of silk and wood flew by my face, pieces torn from one of our wings.

I'd never felt so helpless in my life.

Ahead of me, our engine coughed acrid, black smoke, stinging my nostrils and obscuring my vision. We tilted to port and my stomach told me we were swiftly losing altitude.

More bullets ripped through our wings and fuselage. I ducked down and braced myself as tightly as I could. An image of Sylvie's dark hair and beautiful face flashed in my mind and I knew I'd never have the chance to see my love again.

# Margot

## *July 11, 1958*

**S**omething was terribly wrong and Margot had no idea what else to do.

She'd tried bringing Christophe out of his trance several times, but his mind remained fixed in the past. He continued to relay events concerning a frightening airplane crash during World War I. It had been nearly two hours and the tape was reaching its end. Plus, she knew Christophe's voice would be tired and raw, however, he doggedly clung to his memories. Margot had used every technique she could remember, but none had had any effect on the elderly man. In desperation, she'd even tried slapping his face lightly, but he hadn't reacted at all.

Margot was in a near state of panic when there was a soft knock at the door.

She turned and saw Nurse Blanche enter with a tray of food. Margot knew she must have looked a fright by the nurse's reaction. "Oh! I didn't mean to intrude, Doctor."

"No, Blanche, I'm actually relieved it's you. Come in and close the door."

Blanche did as instructed and set the heavy tray on the table next to the recording machine. Margot turned it off and fumbled with the reels while Christophe continued his slurred narration. "I'm going to need your help sooner than I thought," Margot said. "Christophe is locked in his past and I haven't been able to bring him back to consciousness." Blanche gasped lightly and Margot continued, "I need you to bring a nutrient IV for him, and please ask Dr. Nevins if he will see to my other patients this afternoon so I can stay here and monitor him."

Blanche nodded slowly. "Will he be all right?"

"Physically, yes. As long as we can keep him hydrated and nourished, he should be fine. I think the memories he's suppressed all these years have finally surfaced and he can't, or won't, break free of them now. Once he's relived the experiences, his mind will hopefully let go again and I can bring him back."

"I'll see to it right away," Blanche said, moving to the door. "I'll be back soon with the IV."

Margot did her best to smile. "Thank you, Blanche."

The door closed and Margot let out a pent up breath. She fervently hoped what she'd told the nurse was true. Her nervous fingers finally managed to thread the new tape through the mechanism and she wound it into the empty reel. She started the recording again and sat back with her notebook, watching Christophe's lips move awkwardly around the retelling of his experiences from so many years ago. If time had been their enemy before, it was now a seasoned hunter, expertly moving in for the kill. Once word of Christophe's condition, and her inability to control the situation, reached Dr. Randolph's ears, she knew everything would come to a crashing end — much like the plane Christophe had once rode in.

# Christophe

*July 17, 1918*

The impact happened in stages. I felt the plane level out just before the first jolt from colliding with the earth. We bounced up and glided for several feet before hitting again, much harder the second time.

Brutal cracks sounded through the smoke-filled air; the plane pitched forward, driving the propeller and motor forcefully into the ground. I managed to stay in my cockpit, but slammed painfully into the yoke and wood supports in front of me. The starboard set of wings collapsed and the plane listed to that side, finally coming to rest.

I may have lost consciousness for a short while. The sun had almost completely set by the time I gathered myself enough to crawl out of the ruined aircraft. Somehow, the journal had stayed with me, so I stuffed it in my shirt and made my way to the forward cockpit. I heard another plane buzz somewhere above, but the smoke, still billowing from the engine, veiled the sky. We needed to move quickly before the Germans arrived at the crash site.

Henri still sat in the pilot's seat, head lolled to his right. His cap and goggles had come off either in the air or during the landing. "Captain," I whispered urgently. *"Henri, nous devons aller."* I reached for his face and noticed his eyes were wide open. Startled, I jerked my hand back. Then I saw his bloodied chest. I swallowed the bile that crept up my throat and leaned in for a closer look.

At least one or two of the fighter plane's shots had struck Captain Thibideaux. How he had managed to land us before dying I had no idea, but he earned my eternal gratitude. I hesitated, not knowing what to do or how to pay my respects. Finally, I unhooked the rank insignia from the collar of his uniform and secured it in one of the pockets on my uniform, then I closed his eyelids. Another thought occurred to me and I reached in and removed his pistol from its holster. No sense in letting the Jerries have that, I decided.

Captain Thibideaux had put us down in a narrow field between two substantial groves of trees. The plane's motor had stopped actively belching smoke, though the air around me was still thick with it. I roughly got my bearings from the last light of the sun and decided to head into the southern patch of forest. From the cover of the trees, at least, I couldn't be spotted from the air, but I was sure the Germans would send a ground crew to see what salvage they could garner from the wrecked aircraft. Plus, the Allied armies were south. Only problem was, the Germans were in between me and them.

Feeling well and truly alone, I made my way into the forest.

Darkness descended quickly under the canopy of leaves. Fortunately, the ground was relatively clear of debris as I needed to move as fast as possible. I tried to move lightly and avoid any soft areas to keep from leaving footprints, but in the growing dark, I couldn't tell how successful I was.

My head began to throb and I became dizzy, forcing me to stop and lean on a tree trunk for support. Reaching up, I winced with pain as I felt a tender spot on the left side of my head. The aviator's cap I wore hadn't offered much protection, but at least I was alive.

I bit down my nausea and forced myself forward while the booms of artillery fire echoed across the night. My heart raced each time one of the big guns spoke and my eyes were wide as an owl's, drinking in every bit of light as I picked my way through the woods.

In an effort to calm my nerves, I tried to think logically about my situation. I was behind the German lines, that much was certain, but how far? It had only taken the plane two or three minutes to pass over Chateau Thierry and the Marne, which I knew to be about two miles from our camp. I had only the barest of notions how long we'd been in the air since I'd been concentrating on my drawing, but it was easy for me to imagine we'd gone at least ten to fifteen miles past the river. In our travels, the army often marched up to twenty miles a day, however, that was over open roads in friendly territory.

My logical thinking did a right poor job of calming my nerves.

I drank the last swallows from my canteen which, in my haste, I'd forgotten to fill before we had taken off. I needed to find water, and food, and a place to hole up for the coming day. I'd be too conspicuous moving about in my American uniform during daylight hours.

Some time later I noticed the trees had thinned and soon I came to the edge of this section of forest. The French countryside, as I had seen from the air, held a seemingly random mixture of trees and fields. Likely, the land in front of me would have been cultivated in normal times. As it was, the field was filled with wild grass, ranging from knee to waist height. The moon was up, providing just enough light for me to create a stark silhouette to anyone who happened to cast their gaze in my direction. My head still pulsed with pain, and I hesitated, crouched next to one of the last few trees. The field in front of me would only be the first of many I'd have to cross if I was to make it back to friendly territory.

A shout, or an echo of one, in the distance behind me spurred my tired body forward. I crawled into the grassy clearing, moving with speed, yet taking care to not leave too obvious a trail for someone to follow. My training, back in the States, had included time spent crawling around with heavy packs of equipment strapped tightly across my body. I hadn't understood the purpose of it at the time, but I was appreciative of the practice now. My mind shut down while my body went through the motions necessary to carry me across what I'd guessed to be about two hundred yards of grassland.

As a result, I nearly put my hand on the shell before I realized what it was.

Buried a few inches deep in the soil, the metal casing of an unexploded artillery shell sat directly in my path, lodged in the earth. My heart thudded in my chest as my brain reengaged and I realized what I'd almost done. Many shells failed to explode on impact. Some were duds and harmless. Others, however, only needed a bit of a nudge to set them off. It was impossible to tell one from the other until you caused the thing to blow up.

I pulled my hand back and steadied my breathing. Slowly, my heart receded from my throat and I altered my course through the grass, giving the shell a wide berth. I made it to the next grove of trees without any more surprises and stopped to rest at the base of a stout trunk.

A subtle brightening of the sky told me the short summer night was coming to an end. After considering my limited options, I decided climbing one of the bigger trees and spending the day hiding in the branches and leaves was my best bet. Cautiously, I moved deeper into the forest and found a likely candidate. My boots were not suited for scaling a tree, but I managed to haul myself a good distance up into the sturdy growth and wedge my body tightly between two boughs, reasonably certain I wouldn't fall once I fell asleep. I hadn't addressed my need for food and water, but there was little I could do without exposing myself to dangers far worse than hunger or thirst.

Soon after I settled into a relatively stable position, birds began to chirp around me, hidden in the leaves, greeting the coming dawn. Even they had grown accustomed to the constant barrage of noise the two combatting armies produced, stopping their songs only briefly each time the rapport of a gun or boom of an exploding shell echoed across the fields and trees.

I was bone weary, but sleep eluded me. Unlike my new neighbors, my nerves were too jangled to ignore the blasts of weapons fire sounding with increasing frequency as night became day. Thoughts of my Sylvie, back home on her family's homestead in Montana, crept into my mind once again. Despair settled in next to those memories and I shed tears in the real fear I'd never see her bright face or glowing smile again.

After some time spent in self-pity, I pulled myself together. I still lived. I still drew breath. While my situation was bleak, I still had hope as long as I kept my wits about me. I reached into my breast pocket and carefully pulled out the two letters I'd received from Sylvie since my arrival in France. I was sure she'd written more, but the postal system was less than reliable, especially since we were on the move most of the time. I hoped she had received at least some of the dozen or so I'd sent to her. I opened the first and read, smiling as I always did, at her perfect, even artful, penmanship.

> *Christophe,*
>
> *As I write this, I imagine you are on your ship, sailing off to France. You must write to me as soon as you arrive and tell me all about it! Mama and Papa have told me so many stories of how grand and beautiful it is. I so wish I could see it.*
>
> *Mama is proud of you, I think. She even talks about you*

*once in a while when the two of us are alone. Papa won't, but I*
*think he will come around once you prove to all the world what*
*a hero you are! I smile just thinking about all the wonderful*
*things you will see and do.*

*I miss you so! I keep imagining I see you walking up*
*the road to our house and my heart soars. Then my hopes*
*are dashed when I realize it is just a shadow or trick of the*
*light and I remember where you are. You must come home to*
*me, Christophe! So we can build the life we have talked and*
*dreamed about these past many months. We can marry, and*
*build our house on the land we picked out on the other side of*
*town. We'll have children and you can work on your machines.*
*It will be wonderful I just know it!*

*Oh, here you are, sailing off to war and I am just going*
*on and on about the silliest things! Please take care of yourself*
*and know that I will always love you.*

*Forever yours,*
*Sylvie*

Her romantic ideas of what I'd be doing made me chuckle
softly, especially considering my current predicament. I
remembered the first day our eyes met. I had struck out from
my parents' home in Minnesota when I was seventeen, wanting
to make a life of my own. I'd headed west, not really having
a destination in mind, just desiring to get away. I got on with
my folks fine, but I suppose it was a wanderlust that took hold
of me. I spent a few months exploring the Dakotas, then made
my way into Montana. I came across a bustling railroad town,

called Roundup, and found myself a bed in a boarding house with the intention of investigating any opportunities the railroad might offer. The next day, I'd gone down to the general store to look for a new shirt. While browsing in the store, I kept seeing the ruffles of a homespun dress swirl around the corner away from the aisle I'd just entered. Curious, and a bit mischievous, I reversed my direction and turned the corner. We bumped into each other and I was startled, even though I'd thought to initiate some sort of contact. Her eyes were like smooth chocolate and she smiled shyly with lips that promised to be just as sweet. I think I stammered some sort of apology, then she looked away, still smiling.

I'd spent most of my waking hours after that scheming to somehow meet her again. Luckily for me, her family owned a modest farm a short distance north of town and they visited that store regularly. I found a job assisting an automobile mechanic and saved all the money I could in an effort to impress Sylvie's father that I wasn't a ne'er-do-well. I'd even eventually applied for a homestead in the area.

Then the Army had come calling.

I slid her second letter to the front. It was dated about two weeks later.

> *Christophe,*
>
> *The days just seem to drag on endlessly. I know you have likely only just arrived in France, but it already seems an eternity since you left.*
>
> *It is finally beginning to warm up so Papa can begin the*

*process of planting. I am looking forward to the extra work as I never have before in hopes that I can distract myself from missing you. I even find myself hoping my brothers will tear holes in their clothing, just so I can be at the task of mending them! Isn't that silly?*

*I spoke with an elderly gentleman at church this past Sunday. He said he'd fought for the North in the Civil War, so I'd asked him what it was like, wanting to know more about what you might be doing Over There. He told me the most terrifying stories! I can't even bring myself to write them here. Mama said the old man was probably just trying to frighten me for some twisted pleasure, but Papa, he just scowled — you know the way he does — and walked away.*

*Is it terrible of me to wish for that man to be so evil as to tell me lies just to scare me? I don't know if I could bear it if he were telling me the truth. Is it awful there, my love? Please don't let this War break your spirit! Come back to me whole and healthy so we can put all of this behind us and begin our lives together. I trust in you.*

*Forever yours,*
*Sylvie*

I felt a tear slide down my cheek, but with it, I gained renewed resolve. I had to get back to her, somehow, some way.

The birds around me suddenly stopped their cheerful chatter, even though there had been no disruptive blast of gunfire. The small hairs on the back of my neck stood and I felt my ears straining to gather every little sound.

Only silence greeted me, then I heard something: footsteps on the forest floor.

"*Siehst du etwas?*"

"*Nein.*"

My heart pounded so loud I was sure the whole forest could hear it beating against my ribs. German soldiers moved through the forest below. Paralyzed from necessity and fear, I didn't try to see where they were, but I heard two distinct voices.

"*Was sollen wir tun?*"

"*Augen offen halten.*"

I heard a sigh, then the first one said, "*Es ist besser als zu graben latrinen, ja?*"

The second chuckled in response. "*Ja, sicher.*"

I heard the two pass directly beneath my tree and continue on in the direction I'd been going during the night. I realized I'd been holding my breath and forced my lungs to relax slowly. My heart continued its rapid movement until I heard the first tentative chirping from the birds begin again. If I'd had any spare liquid left in me, I was sure my britches would have been soaked. I'd heard stories about the German prisoner camps and had no desire to experience them first hand. Even that presumed they wouldn't just shoot me on sight.

More sounds of artillery fire boomed in the distance and I resigned myself to the likelihood that I would get very little sleep that day.

# Margot

## *July 11, 1958*

Margot checked the IV tube trailing out of Christophe's arm and noted the bottle was almost empty. She looked at the clock which read half past eight. Dr. Nevins had graciously agreed to see to her other patients without asking why, at least for the day.

She sat back and sighed, then silently admonished herself for making extra noise on the recording. Christophe continued to recount his tale as the machine doggedly passed tape over the recording heads. Surprisingly, his speech actually seemed a little clearer under hypnosis. Frustration over his condition likely made it worse when he was fully conscious.

Quietly, she stood and exited the room. Christophe had remained calm throughout his telling and she needed to replenish the IV. Muscles strained in protest as she worked her way down the hall and her stomach added to her bodily complaints by emitting a loud growl. The facility was still, as if asleep just like the majority of its patients. She raided the dark kitchen for a quick snack, then stopped to pick up two more saline and nutrient bottles before heading back to Christophe's room.

More and more, Margot was convinced that this troubled man was her father, yet she still had no real evidence. Was the Sylvie he talked about her mother? Had he gone back after the war and started the family they had talked about? If so, what had happened? If, in fact, it had been the traumatic events from the war that had triggered his memory loss, why had it encompassed so much of his life after that? Every answered question in Christophe's story only spawned a dozen more. She knew it wouldn't be long before Dr. Randolph would come to check on her progress — especially when he caught wind of recent developments. Margot had a good idea what his opinion of her patient's current state would be, and it wouldn't be favorable. She would certainly lose control of his care, possibly even her job as well if Dr. Randolph decided her incompetence were severe enough.

Christophe stood to lose even more.

She entered the room and found it exactly as she'd left it. After setting the bottles on the table, she saw the tape would also need replacing soon. She listened to his voice and picked up that he was still hiding out behind the German lines, looking for food and water.

Silently, she implored Christophe to hurry.

# Christophe

*July 18, 1918*

**O**nce darkness fell and the chirping of crickets replaced that of the birds, I did what I could to work the blood back into my legs before carefully climbing down the tree. It took several minutes before I felt confident enough to step away from the support of the stout trunk and move on my own.

My stomach had ceased rumbling some time during the day, but now it clenched painfully every few minutes as a less than subtle reminder of its desire for attention. More troubling was the dryness of my mouth and throat. My tongue had cracked and bled, causing it to stick occasionally to the roof of my mouth.

I had to find water at the very least, and soon, or I would save the Jerries the trouble of having to shoot me.

I walked, stumbled, and sometimes crawled through the forest, moving clumsily from tree to tree, largely unaware of the passage of time. Thirst dominated my mind, dismissing my cautious approach from the night before. I kept hold of the need to travel south in the back of my mind, but my sense of direction was muddled at best. My vision was so focused on each tree trunk that I stood dumbly in confusion for several seconds when I encountered another clearing. The moon was bright enough to illuminate a small cottage within the field in soft, gray light.

Once I recognized what the structure was, I made my way forward, uncaring that I might be seen. My only consideration was finding someone who had some water, and possibly food, to share. Dreams mixed with reality and I imagined a warm, quaint house, glowing with a warm yellow light. I even smelled bread, fresh from an oven, and a roast spilling its juices over an open fire. I reached the cottage and leaned against the nearest wall briefly before turning the corner in search of a door.

My dreams were quickly shattered. The whole of the house stood open to the night. Masonry and bits of wood were strewn about in chaotic fashion. The wall I'd seen and a portion of its adjoining neighbor were all that remained standing of the little farmhouse, hit by a stray shell some time in the recent past.

I sank down with my back against the unforgiving stonework in despair. The resolve I'd formed from reading Sylvie's letters during the day blew apart, just like the house had that I leaned against. I looked up, searching the stars for answers, but they remained mute. Only the guns responsible for wrecking this once happy home had anything to say.

My head dropped again, but something caught my eye that I hadn't noticed previously in my dreamy haze: a circular wall of stone about three feet high and wide sat a few yards away from the side of the house.

A well!

Adrenalin surged in me and I scrambled over to the protected hole. A wooden framework supported a hand crank with a slightly frayed rope attached. I also found a bucket lying nearby. After tying the end of the rope to the bucket's handle, I lowered it into the hole and was rewarded a few seconds later with the sound of a muted splash. I anxiously waited for the bucket to sink and fill, then pulled it back up hand over hand from the rope, disdaining the crank. Kneeling in the darkness, I poured cool water into my mouth and guzzled greedily — only to vomit it back up moments afterward. The shock to my system caused me to remember a short session from my army schooling on survival training and dehydration. Going slower, I took a few sips at a time and swirled them around my mouth to keep my confused body from rejecting the life-giving fluid a second time.

I don't know how long I sat there. It took a long time to get my stomach settled and my mind in order. I hadn't realized how much the dehydration had affected me until I'd found some water to drink. My thoughts returned to Sylvie and her letters, safely tucked away in my breast pocket once again. She had saved my life as surely as the well I sat beside. Without her words of encouragement, I seriously doubted I'd have pushed myself as far as I had. I'd have given up and collapsed back in the forest, letting the thirst take me. I made a silent promise then, to her, and myself, to stay strong. No matter how bleak my future seemed.

The moon neared its zenith and I guessed I had no more than an hour, maybe two, of darkness left. The blasted house would offer little protection during the day. Running my eyes across the battered walls, I saw a protrusion of stone blocks, low to the ground, jutting several feet away from the eastern side of the structure. I took another drink from the bucket, filled my canteen, then doused my hands and ran them through my hair and across my face to keep myself alert. After carefully checking my surroundings and not seeing any movement, I forced my body into motion and went to investigate what had caught my eye.

The blocks framed the entrance to a cellar and the doors appeared largely intact. Bending down, I noticed what I thought to be relatively fresh footprints going to and from the cellar. Could someone be in a similar predicament? Maybe one or more of the homeowners survived and had taken refuge under the house. Likely they wouldn't take kindly to an intrusion.

Options were in short supply. Dawn was fast approaching and the amount of artillery fire had definitely increased since the day before. That meant troops were on the move and I could even less afford to remain exposed during daylight hours. I had to take my chances with the cellar. If it was the homeowners, they would be French and happy to see an American, right?

I remembered Captain Thibideaux's pistol and secured it in my right hand. Moving to the left side of the entrance, I grasped the door handle and pulled, using it as a shield. When nothing presented itself, I opened the door the rest of the way and set it quietly on the ground, then peered inside. Stone steps led down into pitch darkness where the moon's faint light couldn't reach.

No sound loud enough to be heard over the guns in the distance reached my ears, so I took a deep breath and crouched through the opening.

My boot scuffs came overly loud to my straining ears and I stumbled slightly from a loose stone on the third step. Gathering myself, I searched the darkness below me in vain. My body blocked what little light there was to see. I took two more cautious steps down and stopped again. An unwelcome, but familiar, odor of unwashed bodies and other less pleasant smells invaded my nostrils, causing my throat to clench.

"*Salut*," I said, then coughed. "*Je suis Américain. Je m'appelé Christophe.*"

I listened carefully, but heard no response. I hesitated a few more seconds before descending once more.

Half a dozen more steps brought me to the bottom and I felt packed dirt rather than stone under my feet. The darkness in front of me was complete and the distasteful smell much stronger. My nose wrinkled reflexively.

I took a step back, whether from instinct or blind luck I'll never know, and avoided the worst from a shovel swung at my head. The metal spade slammed into my left shoulder hard enough to knock me into the earthen wall of the stairwell. I staggered and fell onto the steps.

A figure stepped into the dim shaft of moonlight, no longer blocked by my body. I immediately recognized the German infantry uniform, though it bore signs of heavy use and disrepair. A youthful face, much like my own, stared back at me, eyes wide and full of hatred and fear. He grimaced and raised the shovel to strike again.

I ducked and dove past him farther into the cellar, landing on cool, hard earth. I heard his weapon strike the wall with a metallic thud and he muttered a curse. Rolling onto my back, I saw his form silhouetted in the frame of the stairwell. Grunting, he came at me again.

Suddenly, I remembered the pistol in my hand and brought it up in front of me.

I don't recall pulling the trigger, but the rapport cracked through the enclosed area and the muzzle flash briefly illuminated my attacker's shocked face. The image of his hollowed cheeks and wild eyes burned into my mind.

His momentum carried him forward and he landed heavily on top of me, forcing the air from my lungs. Real or imagined, I felt his breath on my cheek. Unable to scream, I turned and pushed away in panic. The German's body fell away and I coughed heavily, forcing my lungs into action once more.

The cellar was silent except for my labored breathing. A sliver of light from the stairs caught the tip of one of my assailant's boots, which lay motionless in the dirt. Dust from our brief scuffle floated lazily through the moonbeam in contrast to the furious beating of my heart.

I pushed myself up to my knees and held the gun unsteadily, pointed in the direction of the German soldier.

"*Est-il mort?*"

Startled by the sound, I spun, waving the pistol blindly in

front of me. "Who's there? *Qui est là?*"

A frail, unsteady voice asked, "*Vous êtes Américain?*"

"*Oui,*" I confirmed.

I heard a rattled sigh. "*Dieu merci!*" the voice said in relief. He, for it sounded to me like an elderly man, continued to thank God in hushed tones, in between soft coughs.

I turned back to check on the German. His boot remained still in the moonlight shining from the entrance. I fell back on my rear and leaned against the cool earth wall of the cellar. My hands started to shake and I dropped Captain Thibideaux's gun in the dirt beside me.

I killed someone.

The realization struck and my stomach lurched. The German soldier had clearly been close to my age. In another time and place, we might have been friends — played cards, shared a beer.

I killed him.

My rational mind knew he'd been intent on ending my life, but that thought didn't change the outcome of our encounter. Hiding down here as he was, I guessed it likely he'd been a deserter. I imagined him, frightened beyond reasoned thoughts; he'd run away from the horrors he witnessed going on all around him. I would never find out what had really brought him to this place — what had driven him to desperation.

He was dead.

A gentle hand touched my shoulder and I discovered tears dripping from my cheeks. The old man patted me and whispered his thanks. I touched his hand in appreciation, then abruptly had to turn away as my stomach heaved, spilling much of the water I'd drunk from the well outside and creating a muddy mess on the dirt floor. I retched twice more, each time seeing the boy's face in my mind as my muscles clenched painfully. Try as I might, I could not expel the image from my vision.

I sat back again, breathing heavy. The smell of the place registered in my senses again and my stomach threatened more mutiny. I crawled to the steps, regained my feet and started climbing.

I needed fresh air, daylight be damned.

The ethereal gray light of the moon was slowly being replaced by the stark gray light of pre-dawn. I reached the top of the stairs and breathed deep. The familiar booms of heavy guns found my ears like an unwelcome relative come for a visit. I dropped to my knees and fought to regain control of my emotions.

Not long after, the old man crept up the steps behind me and I heard him take several deep breaths. I shuddered to think of how long he'd been trapped below with his German captor.

I turned to look at him. Flesh hung loosely from his face and hands, but I had to revise my first estimation of his age. In the dark, I had conjured pictures of my grandfather when the man had spoken, but I realized this man was probably scarcely older than my father. His brown hair had a touch of gray at his temples and was coated in a fine layer of dust from the cellar. He crouched down and put a hand on my shoulder again and offered a smile that didn't reach his red, puffy eyes.

He then began to relay his story. Groups of German soldiers had visited his family's farm several times, but had left them alone, only taking water from the well and occasionally some food. Four days before, an explosion had rocked the house while he'd been out tending to their small flock of sheep. His wife had been in the kitchen preparing a noon meal and had died instantly. The man's daughter, Helene, survived the blast, but had been injured. Not knowing what else to do while grieving for his wife, but still needing to care for his daughter, they gathered what supplies they could and holed up in the cellar — only venturing out for water. Yesterday, the German deserter had happened upon their hideout. Fearing for his daughter, the man offered to help the distraught young soldier and agreed to share the cellar.

During the telling of his tale, I gathered my wits. Dawn was upon us and we needed to get back underground, in spite of the wretched odor it was the only place we would be relatively safe for the day. Once night fell, we could see about possibly heading south again. First, though, we needed more water.

I got up and made my way to the well. I dropped the bucket in and hauled it back up as fast as I could. Afterward, I jogged unsteadily back and met the man at the top of the stairs, ushering him down. Pulling the door shut behind me, I braced myself for the smell and moved carefully down, trying not to slosh the water from the bucket.

The stench was as powerful as I'd remembered and soon the dead German would add to it significantly. I thought about hauling his body outside, but feared its discovery by a chance passerby, or German patrol, might lead to further investigation of the property.

I set the bucket near the foot of the stairs and groped in the dark for the body. I jumped when my hand contacted his pant leg, then steeled myself to the grisly task of moving the soldier to the far side of the cramped room, so at least we wouldn't be regularly tripping over the corpse.

I found the edge of the space with my hands and crawled over to the body. Thankful for the darkness, I dragged the unfortunate deserter to the side as far as possible. Feeling my way back to the entrance, I located the bucket and asked the man how his daughter was doing, suddenly thinking it strange that I hadn't heard anything from her.

He indicated that she was resting, but could probably use a drink of water. I heard him fumble around briefly, then a bright flare of light caused me to wince and shut my eyes. He apologized and said he'd been saving the lantern since it was running low on oil.

I blinked a tear away and saw the figure of a young woman propped up in the corner a few feet away. Her long dark hair immediately reminded me of Sylvie.

"*N'est-elle pas belle?*" the man asked.

My eyes cleared further and my heart clenched. The woman was indeed beautiful, as her father had just said. She was also just as dead as the German on the other side of the room.

Her injury had been abdominal, possibly a piece of shrapnel

from the house as it had blown apart. Blood had soaked the lower portion of her dress and the earthen floor of the cellar beneath her, creating a dark, foreboding circle.

I turned to her father as he held the lamp and gazed with love at the last of his family. His eyes sparkled and I understood he was seeing her as she had been, not as she was. Somewhere in the ordeal, his mind had broken, and he'd carried on as if his daughter were still alive, not accepting she'd shared the same fate as his wife.

I reached for the lantern and doused the flame. I couldn't bear any more. I sympathized with this man's flight into fancy. Reality had become too painful to accept.

Crawling back to the steps, I found the bucket and washed my face and drank. How much more could my mind take before I lost touch with the world like this poor man? I had worked on the front lines at Verdun, hauling ammunition and assisting the gunners who continually bombarded the German lines. A shell just like one of those had hit the house that had stood a few feet above my head. How many lives had been snuffed out in similar fashion? I hadn't really considered what the results of those gun blasts might be before. We were simply fighting against the Jerries. They weren't people; they were the enemy.

I curled up on the cool dirt floor, praying to God to deliver me safely to my Sylvie one day very soon, and eventually I fell asleep to the muffled lullaby of artillery raining destruction on foe and friend alike.

# Margot

*July 12, 1958*

**M**argot's head jerked and she realized she had just nodded off. Looking up at the clock, she saw it was 6:45 — almost time for the staff to be serving breakfast for the patients.

Christophe continued to recount his harrowing tale of the war and his voice remained remarkably strong. Margot had wet his lips with a damp cloth several times during the night and squeezed a few drops of water in his mouth to help his tongue and throat. Killing the German soldier had obviously affected him greatly and Margot had seen cases of patients severely traumatized for less shocking incidents. Yet, she felt the encounters Christophe spoke of were only a part of whatever horror had broken his mind.

She checked the tape and IV and estimated about an hour left for each before she'd have to tend to them.

*Is he my father?* That question had danced around her thoughts throughout her time at his side. If he was, what would it mean? For her and for him. She'd spent most of her thirty-six years steeped in the belief that she would never meet her parents. Foster care had been loving and mostly agreeable for her, unlike many orphans who never knew of a caring, healthy home life. But, to have contact with her own flesh and blood carried a different meaning entirely. It created a whole new sense of belonging, of family, that she'd never really felt before.

A knock at the door interrupted her musings and an orderly named Raul stepped inside with a tray of dishes. "Oh, I'm sorry doctor! I didn't know you were here."

Margot gave him a tired smile. "It's all right, Raul. You can set that here on the table. Thank you." The aroma of warm oatmeal, gently spiced with a bit of cinnamon, reached her nose and set her stomach to growling.

"Of course, Señora," he said. "Do you need anything else?"

"Do you know when Blanche is working today?"

He shook his head. "I don't, but I can tell her you're looking for her if I see her."

"Thank you."

Raul smiled and left to continue his task of feeding the other patients, pushing a heavily laden cart down the hall. Margot closed the door and eyed the oatmeal and a small bowl of fruit sitting next to it. She smiled ruefully and gave in to temptation. *No sense in starving myself,* she decided, taking the spoon in hand.

She savored the warm meal, but she couldn't set aside her troubling feelings that she and Christophe were running out of time. How much longer would it be before Dr. Randolph discovered her experiment run amok and put an end to it?

For his part, Christophe was still deeply immersed in his past, completely oblivious to the growing danger in his present.

# Christophe

*July 18, 1918*

**A** single gunshot shocked me awake, heart racing. Seconds of panic followed as I tried to recall where I was.

Slowly, I remembered my circumstance. No further sound disturbed the pitch black of the cellar and I began to think I'd dreamed it. I crawled in the direction I thought would lead me to the elderly man and soon brushed against his boot and pant leg.

"*Monsieur?*" I said quietly. He didn't respond so I moved closer.

My hand encountered something wet and warm on the ground and I jerked back in surprise. Cautiously, I brought my hand close to my nose and even over the stench of decay in the cellar I smelled it.

Fresh blood.

"*Monsieur!*" I shouted, grabbing his leg. Feeling his body shift, I had a moment of elation, but the movement was only the settling of his corpse to the floor.

I patted around my waist, then I realized I'd left Captain Thibideaux's pistol laying in the dirt after killing the German.

In the aftermath of discovering the daughter's fate, I hadn't thought to look for it. Carefully, I searched around the farmer's body. After several minutes, I discovered the gun resting near the elderly man's right hand, mired in a slowly expanding pool of blood.

Unsure of what to do, and trying to quell the rising sense of horror within me, I suddenly remembered the lantern the farmer had lit briefly before. Though I dreaded shedding light on what was surely a gruesome scene, I needed to see to retrieve and clean the pistol, and find out if any food was still stored in the cellar.

The search was agonizingly slow, but I finally located the oil lantern, feeling by its weight that it was indeed very low on fuel. Still, some light was better than no light. The matches proved even more difficult until I thought to check the farmer. I was glad of the dark as I felt over the dead man. I discovered a handful of them in his shirt pocket and fumbled with them before striking one against the stone wall.

The match flared to life, showing me nothing but death.

I sat on my knees, frozen by the sight until the match burned down to my fingers. It died out as I flung it away in pain. Collecting myself, I reluctantly struck another and lit the lantern.

The elderly farmer — I hadn't even had a chance to learn his name — lay crumpled to one side, his head and neck a dark red mess. Some time while I slept, he must have come to his senses, at least enough to comprehend the reality of his daughter's condition. Whether he then sought the gun, or stumbled upon it, I would never know. I closed my eyes in grief, then went about my grisly tasks.

In the corner near his daughter, I found two jars of jerked meat. Immediately, I opened one and shoved a strip in my mouth, chewing the tough flesh just enough to choke it down my throat. The rest I stuffed into the several pouches about my person. One of the jars I kept to carry extra water.

The daughter's resemblance to Sylvie struck and disturbed me again. I paused to close her eyes which had remained open in death.

The lantern flickered, telling me my time was short. I crossed back to the farmer and retrieved Captain Thibideaux's pistol, which had claimed yet another life. Having nothing else to use, I wiped off as much of the blood as possible on the old man's shirt, offering a silent prayer as I worked. I stowed the weapon in my belt, then went to the stairs to grab the bucket of water.

My eyes landed on the dead German on the far side of the horrific cellar. Too late, I realized I might have used his uniform as a disguise, even in its dilapidated state. Now, however, it was soaked in his blood and would not serve as protection or deception. I prayed for him as well, wishing him the peace he'd missed in this world.

Taking the bucket, I climbed the stairs and slowly opened the door.

A wave of cool, fresh air washed over me — a sharp contrast to the foulness I was leaving behind. A handful of stars twinkled in a darkening sky and I felt a small glimmer of hope for the first time in more than a day. If anything, the heavy gun fire in the distance had intensified over the intervening hours, but the area around the broken farm seemed still and quiet.

After quietly shutting the door, I crept back to the well and lowered the bucket, eating another piece of meat while I waited. I couldn't tell if it was beef or venison, but it didn't matter. My belly tore into it as if it had been prepared by the finest chef in Paris. I retrieved the bucket and filled the jar I'd taken. Then, I topped off my canteen before having a long drink from the bucket itself. Finally, I soaked the edge of my shirtsleeve and tried to scrub away more of the blood from Captain Thibideaux's pistol. After checking the action to make sure it operated smoothly, I replaced it in my belt and took stock of my surroundings.

Heading south once more, I entered another grove of trees, faintly hoping distance would help fade my memories of the last several hours.

Images of Sylvie mixed uncomfortably with those of the farmer's daughter — Helene, I remembered he'd said her name was — in my mind as I trudged through the forest in the dark. Helene's fate had been undeserved. A random act of destruction had stolen her life, along with her mother's, and her father had then taken his own, unable to handle the grief. Thinking on his decision, I wasn't sure I could disagree with it. I'd been taught that life was precious, and it was a sin to take your own. Cowardly. But the horrors that man had been put through, just in the span of a few days, would try the soul and conviction of anyone. Only a person with the resolve and patience of Job could be asked to bear such burdens and continue on with life.

Even then, the scars would last forever.

I picked my way around the trees, haunted by my thoughts and memories, for an hour or more, finally coming to another clearing. The sounds of fighting were closer now. I heard the pops and cracks of small arms fire, mixed with the continuous barrage of the heavy guns. A thin layer of clouds had moved in, covering the moon and stars like a gauzy veil. A field of tall grass before me stretched far into the distance, unlike the others I'd encountered. Nearby, I spied a trench running almost perpendicular to the southern path I'd chosen. At least one of the warring armies had made its mark on the land, and probably one or both would cross this ground again, such had been the fluid nature of the battle lines throughout France.

The open space between trenches on the battlefield was known as "no man's land." No man could cross that zone in comfort or safety. Any attempts were usually met with violent resistance.

To continue my journey south, it appeared I would have to venture through at least one, and probably several, of those treacherous areas.

I kept myself hidden among the trees, chewing on more of the tough meat, while I considered my options. I wasn't sure where I was, though I decided it likely I was still behind the German lines. I thought our aerial reconnaissance had probably been a prelude to a new assault by the Allied forces, but just where that push had occurred or how successful it had been were a mystery to me. In truth, the outcome was, in all likelihood, still undecided. The dugout stretching out before me appeared unoccupied, but I knew that could change in a short period of time.

Indecision and fear paralyzed me for several minutes. Eventually, I made up my mind to investigate the trench. It would provide me cover, as it was designed to do, and the thought came to me that a too-hasty soldier might have left behind something useful. Food, tools, or even a weapon or ammunition could make a big difference in the success of my quest to rejoin my compatriots.

Scanning the open space a final time, I scurried past the last few trees and dropped into the trench. The sounds of weapons fire continued to echo above and around me, but the close earthen walls gave me a small sense of security. I moved in a slight crouch, making sure to keep my head below the top of the deep furrow.

I made it forty or fifty yards before I saw the first body.

It was face down in the dirt. The uniform looked French, but it was so caked with mud, in the dark, I couldn't be sure. There were several more scattered along the length of the trench. I'd seen enough death to last me forever since I'd arrived in France, so I hurried along, disdaining to investigate the unfortunate men for supplies I might use. I guessed they hadn't been dead overly long, otherwise the smell in the confines of the dugout would have been overpowering. In fact, it smelled almost sweet.

I stopped in my tracks and fumbled for my gas mask. In my panic, I dropped it after I'd pried it free of the canvas and leather case. Finally, I managed to strap it on and took deep breaths of filtered air.

That's when I noticed the prickly, burning sensation on my hands.

I scrambled up the wall of the trench, slipping twice. Once over the top, I crawled away through the tall grass with urgency. Remembering the jar I'd filled with water, I stopped and used all of it to wash my hands before continuing on, cursing my stupidity. Before long, my lungs were laboring too hard to keep going, though whether from the gas or simply the exertion of breathing through the mask I didn't know.

Mustard gas got its name from its odor — a sweet, flowery smell — and it could remain potent for days after employment, depending on the weather conditions. In daylight, I might have noticed the telltale dark blistering on the bodies, but in my haste, and at night, I hadn't seen the danger.

I flopped back in the grass, my chest heaving. I took a chance and lifted my mask, testing the air. The smell of dry earth, along with my own unpleasant odor, reached my nostrils. I pulled the mask off the rest of the way and struggled to calm my breathing. Only time would tell if I'd inhaled enough of the poisonous gas to kill me.

Looking up at the sky, I saw a light spot in the clouds where the moon tried to shine through. I wondered what Sylvie was doing, right at that moment. Was she gazing into the heavens, thinking of me? My vision grew fuzzy as tears welled in my eyes. Coughing, I rolled over and dug a piece of the jerked meat from its pouch and ate it. My body had been stretched to its limits and beyond. Not for the first time, I despaired I would never see her again — my Sylvie. Above me, the clouds moved in a slow, stately dance. I imagined the two of us spinning, arm in arm, in the wheat fields near her family's home. We laughed and kissed and spun some more until we were too dizzy to stand any longer. In a heap on the ground, we held each other, gazing up at the clouds while our dizziness faded away …

I must have lost consciousness. I remember it being brighter, then a shadow moved to cover me.

"Sarge! Over here! It's one of ours."

I heard footsteps come close. "Huh, what do you suppose he was doin' out here?"

I tried to speak but could only croak and cough.

"He's alive! Get a medic over here!"

# Margot

*July 12, 1958*

Margot listened as Christophe relayed his experiences after his discovery by the U.S. soldiers. He was taken to a nearby army medical facility and treated for his ailments, including exposure to the mustard gas. She realized the toxic chemicals could possibly account for the mysterious stomach problems he'd mentioned previously. She made a note to do some further research if — no, when — they made it through their current predicament.

She still held to her belief that his mind would come back to the present after he finished reliving his troubled past. But, a hint of doubt crept into her thoughts as she listened to him describe convalescing in the hospital with the other wounded. Surely, the horrific events he'd described had been the catalyst for his memory loss. Who wouldn't want to hide away from such experiences? Yet, Christophe's memory soldiered on, much like the doughboys of the era he described. Margot tried all the techniques at her disposal, that she considered relatively safe for his fractured mind, to bring him back to reality with no success.

A knock at the door startled Margot from her musings. Nurse Blanche entered the room with a look of worry on her face.

Margot smiled with relief. "It's good to see you, Blanche."

"And you, though, if I may say so, Doctor, you look terrible," she offered with a shy smile.

"That doesn't surprise me," Margot said, chuckling. "I need you to do me another favor if you have a few minutes."

"Of course."

"Can you keep an eye on Christophe for me while I go make my rounds? I don't want to ask one of the other doctors to fill in for me again."

Blanche nodded. "How is he doing?"

"The same. He relayed a terrible story about his experiences in World War I, but that episode seemed to come to a close. I had hoped his conscious mind would rise again, but it appears he has more to work through." Margot sighed and opened the door. "I'll be back as soon as I can. Thank you, Blanche."

Margot went straight to the hospital's pharmacy to check on her other patients' medications. All the while, her thoughts were back in Christophe's room. She had felt so sure his conscious mind would resurface after the reliving of his war experience, it came as a shock that he had continued on. Had she made a grievous error in continuing the hypnosis sessions in such rapid succession? Had she let her selfish desires to discover her own past cloud her judgment regarding Christophe's mental health and stability? The possibility weighed heavily on her. The idea that her inexperience, and stubbornness in refusing to seek the help and advice of her colleagues, might have seriously injured someone who had been placed under her care made it nearly impossible to focus on the tasks in front of her. Only her determination to not let one error cause another allowed her to carry on with her duties.

Fortunately, none of her other charges had suffered from her neglect. Silently, she praised the staff for their compassion and attention to detail. The nurses and orderlies, like Blanche and Raul, were the lifeblood of any medical facility. Without them, the place couldn't function.

Speakers in the hallway crackled briefly and Edith's voice rang through the building. "Dr. Braun, please report to Dr. Randolph. Dr. Braun to Dr. Randolph's office, please."

Margot's heart lurched. She'd known she would have to face her superior's scrutiny at some point, but that point had always been in the future. The moment when future became present tore at her insides. Out of options, it was time to face the music.

Taking a deep breath, she strode woodenly toward Dr. Randolph's office, resolved to do whatever was best for her patient.

Never mind that said patient was possibly also her father.

She reached the solid door and knocked before stepping inside. The large windows offered a gloomy view. Heavy, gray storm clouds had moved in during the night, mirroring Margot's knot of emotions. Dr. Randolph sat passively behind his formidable desk, penning notes in a file.

Margot knew better than to speak first, but her nervousness overrode her sense of decorum. "You wished to see me, Doctor?"

His pen hesitated only a moment before resuming its motion. "Sit down, Dr. Braun."

No, "please," Margot noted. That didn't bode well. She perched on the edge of the nearest chair and did her best to wait patiently.

Meticulous to a fault, Dr. Randolph completed his entry, after what felt like an eternity to Margot, and looked up at her. "Would you care to update me on your progress with your Mr. Doe?"

Sure that he was already quite familiar with Christophe's condition, Margot made sure not to fudge any details. "I initiated another hypnosis session yesterday morning, around eleven o'clock. Christophe had complained of bad dreams the night before and was eager to continue exploring his memories. We went back to a time during World War I and discovered he had been a soldier in the war. After the usual amount of time, I attempted to bring him out of the hypnotic state, but failed to do so. He remained trapped in his memory, reliving the whole experience. I called for a nutrient IV, to help keep his physical condition stable, and asked Dr. Nevins to perform my afternoon rounds. I spent the night with the patient, monitoring his condition and periodically attempted to pull him out of the trance, without success. He has related a tale of traumatic experiences, which I believe —"

"Enough," Dr. Randolph said. "While I appreciate your

honesty, I do not have the same admiration for your total disregard of procedure. Why on Earth, when you encountered difficulties in your examination, did you not consult another doctor for his aid and opinions?"

Here, before her, was the crossroads Margot had dreaded reaching. Dr. Randolph had said he appreciated her honesty. So be it. "I believe the patient to be my biological father."

His bushy eyebrows shot up. "Pray, tell me what led you to this astonishing conclusion."

Margot sighed and tried to collect her thoughts. Lack of sleep was catching up with her. "A session we had a few days ago revealed his last name is Poinsette, an unusual name which also happens to be my maiden name. That, coupled with his age and some memories and events from my own past have convinced me the possibility is a strong one."

Dr. Randolph paused, as if waiting for more from her. "That's it? Do you realize how preposterous that sounds, Dr. Braun?"

Margot nodded. "Yes, which is why I had kept it out of my reports. I knew if I had expressed those feelings, you would assign another doctor to his case."

"And rightfully so! Our job here is to be clinical with our guests. Feelings and emotions do not, and cannot, play a part in that."

"With this last session, I had hoped —"

"There is no room for hope! Psychiatry is science, Doctor. It's not about rolling dice and hoping we get it right! Your emotions have led you astray, as I suspected they would. I've assigned Dr. Tate to take charge of the case, immediately."

"What?!" Margot's worst fears had come true and her blood rushed, heating her face.

"Sit down," Dr. Randolph said sternly.

Margot hadn't realized she'd stood, but she ignored his order. "Christophe's condition is precarious. Dr. Tate's heavy-handed approach won't — "

"I've made my decision, Dr. Braun. It's already done."

The implication of that statement sunk in quickly. "No!" Margot turned and ran for the door.

"Doctor!"

She ignored him, slamming the heavy door behind her and running down the bleached hall. Her heart pounding against her ribs, Margot navigated the corridors with practiced feet and arrived breathless at Christophe's door. She turned the knob and burst into the room, seeing Nurse Blanche's startled face.

"Blanche! Has Dr. Tate been here?"

The nurse recovered from her surprise and answered, "He just left saying he needed to prepare a new IV. I'm worried. What does he plan to do?"

Margot breathed a small sigh of relief. She thought it likely he went to mix a potent pharmacological cocktail to replace the simple nutrient and saline solution. Her problem now was how to prevent any tampering with Christophe while he continued his journey through the past. She glanced at the single chair in the room, then at the door. "Blanche, I'm going to ask you to leave. I don't want you to get in trouble."

The younger woman stiffened. "If it's all the same, I'd like to stay."

"I understand and appreciate your commitment to this, but I think you can be of more help on the outside."

"What are you planning to do?"

Margot shook her head. "Just please, step out of the room. And thank you so much for all you've done. I am in your debt."

Blanche hesitated a moment longer, then opened the door and slipped out. Margot checked that the latch held, then wedged the chair firmly under the knob. She kicked the legs toward the door to be sure the fit was as tight as possible. Thankful Christophe hadn't been placed in one of the higher security rooms, which had no knob or handle on the inside, she sat on the corner of his bed and prayed her barricade would be strong enough to allow Christophe the time he needed.

After a few seconds to gather herself, Margot turned her attention to the man whose arrival only a few days before had turned her life upside down. She listened as he recounted the missing events of his life, her practiced ear picking out the words from his stroke-induced slur. Soon, she discovered his scene had shifted. No longer was he on the battlefields of France, but on a small homestead in Montana.

# Christophe

## *September 3, 1921*

**B**one weary from fighting a broken plow, I sat back in the stiff wooden chair on the small porch of our home. Dark red and purple clouds, with no hint of rain, drifted in the sky before me as the sun slowly set in the distance behind our house. Sylvie rested inside, suffering from the ills of a difficult pregnancy. Doc had said the baby was only days away on our last visit and I prayed he was right. I could scarcely bear watching the torment she endured in an effort to bring new life to this world.

Hunger caused my stomach to grumble. Sharp pain followed close on its heels and I pressed my hand against my middle until the sensation subsided.

To say things hadn't gone as planned since my homecoming from the war hardly began to tell the tale.

My encounter with the mustard gas had left me with some minor blistering on my hands and neck, but the real damage had been done inside, which I didn't begin to understand until later. The army's doctors patched me up and eventually sent me back to rejoin my unit. The push north of the Marne River seemed to be a real turning point and the Germans surrendered later in the year. I served with an expeditionary force for a few months before being shipped home early in 1919. After several long, anxious train rides, I arrived back in Montana and held my precious Sylvie in my arms once again. What I had thought would be our happily-ever-after, however, soon turned out to be a time of setback and misfortune.

We did marry, with her parents' blessing, that summer after my return, and took possession of a small homestead not far from Sylvie's family. I had always been more interested in machinery than farming, but we made the decision to try a crop of winter wheat late in November, with anticipation of harvest early the following summer. In the meantime, I found a job working at a livery, in the town of Roundup, performing repairs on buckboards and other equipment. The hours were long and, combined with the work required on our new home and land, it was a difficult life.

Still, I much preferred the backbreaking work of the day over the fears of night.

Regardless of how hard I pushed myself physically while the sun was up, I could not sleep through the night. Often I did not remember the dreams, but would simply wake up screaming and soaked in sweat.

The times I recalled my dreams were worse.

My experiences in the war had left me frightened and hollow, yet I had always felt, once I returned home and distanced myself from the memories, the vividness would fade with time.

The doctor I had spoken to about my nightmares before I left France had even confirmed my hopes. The "shell shock," as he termed it, was a temporary condition and I would recover with rest away from the battlefield.

After more than two years, I felt it was worse, not better. If not for my beloved Sylvie, I surely would have gone mad.

Even with her love and support, I struggled to separate dream from reality at times, during the day as well as the night. Loud noises would set my heart to racing and send me into such a panic that I sometimes forgot where I was. I lost my job at the livery after my behavior so scared an elderly woman, she claimed I was possessed by the devil. I wanted to tell her if I thought an exorcism would rid me of my memories, I'd gladly submit to one.

The pattern repeated itself twice more over the next several months. I would find work only to have it snatched away because of my unreasoned outbursts and fits of confusion. Also, because of my erratic demeanor and my growing inability to hold down a job, Sylvie's parents became increasingly disenchanted with me. Sunday dinners and family get-togethers occurred less and less frequently. I tired of trying to put on a good face and Sylvie tired of defending me. Our relations rekindled briefly when Sylvie became pregnant for the first time that winter of 1919, but soured again when she lost the baby the following spring.

Bad luck and misfortune abounded that spring and summer of 1920. Sylvie was despondent over her miscarriage and heavy spring snows collapsed the roof of her parents' barn, killing two horses and some other livestock. The losses came at a bad time for them and they ended up pulling up stakes and moving south to Wyoming or Colorado — Sylvie hadn't told me where they'd settled and I hadn't asked. Her mother wrote her occasionally, but Sylvie never talked about the letters. I assumed the news was rarely good or she would have shared it with me.

We struggled through that year, growing our own food and finding work wherever we could. Sylvie had some talent for sewing and sold a few dresses in town and to some of our neighbors, while I hired myself out as a handyman for anyone who had a job to do. After her family had moved on, she and I were all each other had. At times, it felt like we were the only two people in the world, isolated in our tiny house, taking care of ourselves. We celebrated Christmas sparsely, as we did with everything, giving each other homemade gifts. She had knitted me a winter scarf with my initials, "CP," on one end. I had collected a sampling of wildflowers throughout the summer and had pressed and dried them, mounting them in a small picture frame I had taken as payment for felling a tree for one of our neighbors. I remembered spending that night, after we'd opened each other's gifts, dreamless and woke thinking it had been the best Christmas present I'd ever had.

After discovering Sylvie was pregnant again in February, the nightmares returned with a vengeance. I spent my nights in the front room, not wanting to keep her awake and worrying over me. It had taken her several months to recover from losing our first child and I was determined to do everything in my power to prevent her from going through that trauma a second time.

"Christophe."

I started at hearing her voice, snatched from my reverie. The clouds I'd been focused on had gone from red and purple to dark gray and a smattering of stars peeked through places where the clouds were too thin to cover them.

"Christophe," Sylvie said again softly from the doorway behind me. "I think it's time."

I turned to look at her as the words registered in my brain. Her dark hair hung limply around her face, which glistened with sweat. The thin dress she wore clung tightly to her moist skin and swollen belly while she leaned heavily on the doorframe for support, giving me a small, pained smile.

She had never looked more beautiful to me than in that moment.

I jumped up and took her by the arms. "Sit here while I hitch up the horse." I placed her gently in the chair I'd just vacated and ran to our small barn. We couldn't afford an automobile — much as I would have liked one — so we had to settle for a carriage of the horsed kind. I had prepared the payload portion of the buckboard a couple of days earlier with all the spare blankets and bedding we had in anticipation of this momentous trip to town.

Finding a match, I struck it and lit a lantern hanging by the door so I could see. Our horse, an elderly mare we named Tess, stamped her feet inside her stall, undoubtedly upset at being disturbed at this late hour.

"Settle down, ole girl," I said. "We've got big doin's and I need you to cooperate."

Whether my words or a hand from above worked on her, I didn't know, nor did I care. I was simply thankful she calmed down enough for me to go about the business of harnessing her up to the wagon in record time. I blew out the lantern and led her and the cart out of the barn.

Sylvie remained where I'd left her on the porch. She had a tense expression on her face when I went to collect her. "What's wrong?" I asked.

She cocked an eyebrow at me, then let out a long breath. "Christophe, love of my life, I am having a baby. Everything is wrong and you can't fix it, so don't even try."

Unsure how to respond, I offered my hand and helped her out of the chair. I started to lead her to the back of the buckboard when she pulled up short.

"I'm not riding back there."

I turned to her, noting the growing darkness made her appear more pale than normal. "But, I thought it would be more comfortable for you to lie down —"

"I'm not riding back there, Christophe."

I opened my mouth to argue, then thought better of it. "At least let me take some of the blankets and make the seat a little softer."

She eyed me, maybe suspecting a trick. "All right, but please hurry."

I dropped her hand and vaulted the side, grabbing the pieces that I thought would offer the best padding and arranged them on the bench. After jumping back down, I moved behind her, holding her by the waist, and lifted her to the seat. She adjusted my makeshift cushions and gingerly sat down. I paused for a moment, to make sure she wasn't going to change her mind, before climbing up and gathering the reins.

The three-mile ride to town was torturous for us both. The reasons were obvious in Sylvie's case. For me, driving by starlight was much harder than I'd imagined, and I cringed at every hole or protruding rock we hit, only able to guess at the agony my beloved bride endured. After what felt like an eternity, we arrived at the hospital.

The building itself was surprisingly large for a town the size of Roundup. The railroad had caused a minor boom in the population and the closest town of any size was the city of Billings, fifty miles or more to the south. Built of solid stone blocks, the hospital had an archway on the southeast corner marking the entrance. I stopped Tess directly in front and handed the reins to Sylvie. As I hopped down, a sharp pain in my gut reminded me I hadn't eaten. Annoyed at my weakness, I massaged the sensitive area with my fist and jogged up to the front door.

On a previous visit, the doctor had shown me a pull chain that rang a bell inside for after hours emergencies. I found it and tugged vigorously. My impatience made the wait interminable, but finally a woman of middle years came to the door and unlocked it.

"Can I help you?"

"My wife has started labor."

The woman peered past me toward the street and our cart. "Bring her in, I'll rouse the doctor."

Thanking her, I ran back to Sylvie and helped her down from the seat. She winced and I gave her a second to collect herself before urging her forward. The woman met us at the door and took Sylvie by the hand.

"I'll take her to the birthing room, why don't you look after your horse and cart?"

I hesitated, not wanting to be apart from my wife, but of course I couldn't just leave Tess standing hitched up to the buckboard out on the street.

The woman smiled thinly, noting my uncertainty. "Just ring the bell again when you've seen to everything. I'll set up a cot in our waiting room for you."

I nodded my thanks and kissed Sylvie.

"I'll be fine," she assured me. "Take care of Tess."

I kissed her again and reluctantly went and climbed aboard our wagon. As I guided Tess deeper into town, I realized I was fortunate this was a Saturday and there were still a few folks out and about, even at that late hour. Prohibition had forced the closure of anything calling itself a "saloon," but there were numerous places for anyone to get a drink that wanted one.

I found a stable reasonably close to the hospital that was also willing to keep an eye on our buckboard after I explained my reason for leaving it. The fellow was pleasant and only charged me for Tess's feed, giving me a clap on the back and wishing me good luck. I thanked him and made my way back to the hospital.

The woman, one of the nurses I discovered, let me back in as she'd promised and directed me to a small waiting area with a few chairs along one wall and a sturdy looking cot across from them. A folded blanket and pillow were stacked neatly on one end.

I spent most of that night pacing the small room like a big cat, caged in a zoo. Intermittently, I heard Sylvie's muffled cries from somewhere down the hall. It took all the self control I had not to run to her at those times. I had been expressly forbidden from her room. The nurse claimed it would only upset her more and distract her from the task at hand. I surrendered, but only from fear that the hospital would turn us out if I didn't do as they asked.

Twice during the night, as I wore a path in the hard floor, my vision clouded and I found myself back in that dark cellar under the ruined farmhouse in France. My heart raced and bile burned my throat. The stench of the place seared my nostrils before I could shake my head and dismiss the too vivid scene. I wondered, not for the first time, if I was going mad. How could I care for my family in such a state? How could Sylvie continue to love a man who'd lost his mind?

The night dragged on, as only one spent in helpless waiting could. By the time the first rays of sunshine made their way through the wavy glass of the only window in the room, I was utterly spent. Nurses sporadically brought me water or coffee, but said little. I guessed they wanted as little to do with the raving lunatic roaming their waiting room as possible. I'm quite sure I looked the part. Soaked with sweat, unshaven, and occasionally grimacing in pain from my abused insides, I can only imagine what they thought of me.

Exhausted, I took a break from my pacing and sat on the edge of a chair, staring at the dust motes floating serenely through the sunbeam that lit the room. It was almost like seeing stars. Most were small and indistinct, while a few were large and sparkled brightly. Images of a night sky, half a world away, danced briefly before me, like afterimages from a photographer's flash powder. The sounds of gunfire, and even the screams of wounded men, echoed through my scattered thoughts.

"Mr. Poinsette?"

I blinked and struggled to remember where I was. Someone moved close to me.

"Mr. Poinsette? Would you like to meet your daughter?"

My daughter? My daughter! I stood up like a shot, startling the poor nurse who held a bundle of blankets in her arms. Shaking my head, I mumbled an apology.

The nurse offered me a small smile and leaned in closer, opening the blanket a fraction. Inside, I saw a puffy, red face, with eyes firmly closed and a tuft of dark brown hair curled on her forehead. A giddy feeling welled up inside me and spread a broad smile across my face. "She's beautiful," I croaked.

"The doctor says she seems quite healthy and normal," the nurse said. I nodded, but couldn't take my eyes off the bundle she held. "Do you have any family here to help out for a while?"

Her question roused me from my trance. "Yes. Well, no, they're not here. I'll have to send a message. My parents offered to come stay with us for a time when the baby arrived."

"Oh, and where do they live?"

"Minnesota. A few miles from Worthington."

"That will be a long trip. There's a telegraph office just a couple of blocks from here if you'd like to let them know."

"Thank you, I'll do that."

"I'd better get her back and see if she'll nurse. Oh! I almost forgot. Have you picked a name?"

I nodded. "We're naming her after Sylvie's grandmother, Margot."

# Margot

## July 12, 1958

**"D**r. Braun!" Dr. Randolph's gruff voice was muffled by the closed door, but Margot clearly heard his irritation through the barricade. "This is your final warning. I have the fire department here, ready to break down the door. Open up now, before this comes to property damage!"

*Yes,* Margot thought, *because property damage is certainly the most important issue at hand here.* Dr. Randolph had been at it for the better part of an hour, trying to talk her out. Instinct told her Christophe was close to something important, but she'd run out of ideas to stall Dr. Randolph. Now it appeared her time was at an end.

In desperation, she tried one final tack. "Doctor, I'm Christophe's next of kin and I want him released from this facility."

"Dr. Braun, you mentioned your belief in my office. The notion is preposterous."

"He confirmed it through the hypnosis just moments ago." Margot's heart had fluttered out of control when she'd heard

Christophe announce the name of his newborn daughter. She knew beyond a shadow of a doubt in her mind this man was her father.

"A confirmation you fervently wish for which could have easily been insinuated in his thoughts. No, we're not going down that road." There was a brief pause, then she heard, "Break it down."

Seconds later, an axe head split the sturdy wood of the door, sending splinters flying. Margot turned and shielded Christophe with her body. The fireman worked the axe free and struck again, widening the hole.

# Christophe

*September 4, 1921*

"**N**urse, how is my wife? Can I see her?" I asked, still disoriented from the realization that this was my child, bundled up before me.

"Not yet." The nurse frowned slightly. "She still has to deliver the afterbirth and is having some difficulty. The doctor is working with her now."

"What? What does that mean?"

"I'm sure everything will be fine." Her expression said otherwise and I felt a wave of panic rising in me. I looked down the hallway, searching out which door might be hers.

"Mr. Poinsette, wait. The doctor is doing everything he can."

A scream of pain and terror ripped through the building, causing my chest to freeze. I brushed past the nurse and ran.

"Mr. Poinsette!"

I heard shouting ahead of me and located the source. Throat tight, I flung the door open.

The color red washed over me, burning itself in my mind. I hesitated, trying to grasp the scene before me. Blood-soaked sheets covered the bed. The doctor, also awash in blood, turned to me with a surprised, haunted look in his eyes. I shouldered him aside and saw her.

The love of my life, who had given me the strength to carry on when I'd lost all hope, stared back at me with dark, vacant eyes.

I became a man of two worlds in that instant. In both of them, I saw a young, bloody woman whose life had been cruelly extinguished — one lying in a dark, earthen cellar, the other in a sterile hospital bed.

My light had been snuffed out.

Darkness ruled me.

# Margot

*July 12, 1958*

**"S**sssylvieeeeee!" Christophe's anguished cry burst from his throat, startling Margot and causing the men surrounding her to pause.

The door had given way after several more applications of the axe. Margot still sat on the edge of the bed, shielding her patient and father, while the fireman, Dr. Randolph, and Dr. Tate shouldered their way into the small room.

Christophe sat up with a wild look and Margot placed her arm across his chest.

"Get him sedated and restrained," Dr. Randolph said.

Dr. Tate stepped forward, hypodermic in hand.

"No!" Margot shouted. "He's just come out of the trance and he's disoriented."

"Dr. Braun?" Christophe asked. His eyes relaxed a bit.

"Yes, it's me. I'm here."

"Dr. Braun, move aside and let Dr. Tate see to his patient."

"I don't undahssstand," Christophe said to the men. "Dr. Braun isss taking care of me."

"Not any longer," Dr. Randolph said flatly. "Her selfish, negligent actions have placed your health at risk. Dr. Tate will be seeing to your needs now."

"By keeping him constantly sedated?" Margot interjected. She turned to Christophe. "Do you remember? I know it was hard to experience, but do you remember now what you went through?"

Christophe's eyes searched the room, then cast down to his lap. "Yesss." His right hand covered his face and he began to sob. "Yessss. I remembah. My Sssylvie."

Dr. Randolph sighed. "Dr. Braun, it may be impossible to reverse the damage you've done. He may never be able to distinguish his own real memories from ones you have unwittingly implanted in him."

"I didn't implant anything!"

"Maybe not consciously, but intent is not necessary for a crime to be committed."

"Crime?! All I've done is help him!"

"I have no doubt you believe that." Dr. Randolph shook his head. "More evidence that women should not —"

A shout came from the hall. "Dr. Randolph!"

Annoyed at the interruption, he turned to the speaker. Margot looked up and saw Blanche's youthful face. She spared a glance in Margot's direction before addressing the hospital director. "Christophe has a visitor."

"What? Who?" Dr. Randolph stuttered.

A middle aged woman stepped into view, peering through the

ruins of the doorway. Wavy, brown hair hung loosely around her face as she searched the crowded space. When her eyes landed on Christophe, they widened in recognition. "Christophe!"

"Laura?" Christophe looked up and asked, his voice shaking.

She answered by pushing past the confused men and rushing to the bed. Margot quickly stood to make room. Laura hugged him fiercely and Christophe returned it with his strong right arm, his hand still wet with tears darkening the back of her blouse.

More movement in the hallway caught Margot's attention. She looked up and saw Hal's tired face grinning back at her. Joy and relief flooded through her once the full realization of what had taken place hit.

"Who is this woman?" Dr. Randolph recovered enough to ask.

"Laura Poinsette," Margot answered. "Christophe's wife." She then stepped around the two dumbfounded doctors and met Hal in the corridor after giving a smile to Blanche.

"Looks like I missed a good party," Hal said with a smirk.

"I only throw the best," Margot said, putting her arms around him. "What took you so long?"

# Margot

## *September 4, 1958*

Margot took a deep breath and blew out all the candles on the cake, to the claps and cheers of her gathered family and friends.

"You've got a good pair of lungs there," Hal teased.

Margot chuckled. "Won't be long before one breath won't be enough. I think you spent more money on candles than the cake!"

"The clerk at the dime store thought I was stocking up a bomb shelter," Hal replied with a wink. "What did you wish for?"

"I can't tell you or it won't come true! Besides," she said, looking around their crowded dining room and parlor, "I think I've used up all my wishes for a lifetime."

Christophe — her father, she was still getting used to that — sat in one of their comfortable chairs by the radio, talking with a friend he'd made at the local senior center. No doubt they were trading war stories. Christophe had embraced his memories, although they still troubled him, he found he preferred to deal with any unpleasantness rather than have his life be simply a void. Margot knew he faced more struggles ahead, but acceptance was a big first step.

With the information on the recordings, she had been able to reconstruct some of the missing details after her birth. She had contacted the hospital in Montana and received copies of their records. After discovering Sylvie's death, Christophe had lost all control, becoming violent with the staff and had to be confined and sedated. From the information he had given the nurse, they contacted his parents who came and collected the newborn Margot. Christophe was deemed too dangerous to be allowed to leave, even after protests from his mother and father. Reluctantly, they returned to Minnesota with the baby, leaving Christophe in the hospital's care. Sedatives of the time were largely opium based, which created additional problems for him in the form of addiction, and could have contributed to his memory loss as well. It wasn't until several years later that he had been considered stable enough to be on his own, and by then his mother and father had both passed away. Knowing Christophe was in no condition to care for a child, the doctors made the decision to keep the knowledge of Margot's existence to themselves, after determining that he had no recollection of the event.

That omission had initially angered Christophe when Margot had presented the information to him several days before. She forced herself to admit similar feelings, but soon realized the doctors' intentions had been good, and her life, at least, had probably been the better for it.

Even though she had been right about Christophe, Margot's actions still had led to losing her job at the hospital. She hadn't been surprised and part of her even welcomed the result. After a little more than a month of searching, she'd found a position at a retirement home not far away. The pay was less, but she and Hal would manage.

The front door opened and Margot saw a flushed Laura step inside, followed by a bounding Misty, who enveloped her father in a big hug. Laura smiled at Christophe, then turned to Margot. "I'm sorry we're late! I was unpacking boxes and lost track of time."

Margot smiled and cut a slice of cake. "It's no trouble. Cake?"

Misty appeared in front of Margot. "Yes, please!" Laura and Margot shared a laugh.

After having no family for so long, it was still hard for Margot to wrap her mind around the one that had been thrust upon her. Laura was technically her step-mother, even though she was only a few years older than Margot, and Misty was her half-sister, who was young enough to be Margot's daughter. Frank, Laura's son from her previous marriage, had joined the military, after some troubled teenage years, and was serving in Okinawa. He had been surprised at all the developments, but had wished his mother and sister the best.

Laura and Misty made the decision to reunite with Christophe after spending several days with him upon their arrival. Laura had found a job at a local department store just a couple of weeks before and had been busy making the move from Nebraska. Fortunately, Laura had gone to visit her parents the day Hal showed up to try to convince them to let him know of her whereabouts. She had somewhat reluctantly decided to talk with the hospital and Christophe, but when Hal couldn't reach Margot by telephone, his intuition had told him there was trouble. He had squeezed Laura and Misty in the cab of his truck, and the three of them drove straight through, arriving just in time.

Margot served slices of cake and cups of lemonade to the rest of their guests, and then, once everyone was happily enjoying their sweet snack, she leaned against the dining room wall and reflected on the whirlwind of a summer that had left her life so changed. New friends, and new family that she would cherish the rest of her days, talked and laughed, filling her home with love and warmth.

She caught her father's eye across the room. He gave her a quick wink and a smile that seemed even to spread to the slack left side of his face. Then she felt Hal's arm slip around her waist, his strong hand gripping her tight.

"Happy Birthday," he whispered with a smile of his own.

# Christophe

## *September 4, 1958*

I glanced up and noticed Margot looking at me with a grin of satisfaction from the corner of the room. I winked back and smiled, suddenly overcome with joy. My daughter — Sylvie's daughter — had grown into a beautiful and accomplished woman. Her husband, Hal, gave her a hug and whispered something in her ear.

"Are you going to finish your cake, Papa?"

I turned and saw Misty's sweet, yet greedy eyes on the plate in my lap. I chuckled. "Yesss, I am, you ssscamp."

Her bottom lip puffed out, but only briefly before she smiled and leaned in to kiss my cheek. I barely felt the touch of her lips on the left side of my face. She reached up with her hand and stroked the spot she'd kissed.

"Your skin feels funny."

I nodded. "It probably doesss. The mussscless don't work right anymore." My speech had gotten somewhat better the past few weeks, but I still had a distinct slur that would likely never go away. My mind had been made whole again, but my body was a wreck that couldn't be salvaged. Yet, if the trade was necessary, I'd have gladly made it again. My memories still haunted my dreams, but they belonged to me and I had no desire to give them up again.

I looked into Misty's face and saw much of Laura there. "Why don't you sssee if Margot needsss any help cleaning up? Ssshe might have sssome more cake leftovah."

Her eyes sparkled and she made her way to the dining room. At fourteen, she was as tall as Laura and showing signs of becoming a woman. My heart clenched with regret at the years of watching her grow up I'd missed.

Laura sat next to me and put a hand on my knee. "She's already got her eye on a boy in the apartment building."

I groaned. "Did you get thingsss ssettled at the ssschool?"

"Yes, she starts next week."

I paused, then found her eyes, trying to gauge her mood. "Thank you for coming. For making the move."

She smiled. "I never stopped loving you. I just didn't know how to cope with your secrets." She reached over and took my right hand. "I'm sorry for what happened. And I'm sorry for all the time we've lost."

My vision blurred and I blinked away a tear. "I'm the one who'sss ssssorry." I squeezed her hand. "But, no more looking back. We live here, and now."

She nodded her agreement and kissed me. Her lips were just as I remembered them.

"Are you going to finish your cake?" she asked.

I laughed.

# Afterword — A Story Twice Lived

**T**o the story! I felt his pain but I could do nothing about it. As I aged, from two years old and still just a kid, standing up or running away seemed to be no solution to his temper tantrums. I began taking his pain as a way of accepting his quick flare up over any provocation. I knew he had a pain in his "tummy", but I didn't recognize his fears of the unrelenting trauma scenes that came as an aftermath of the battle experiences. My father was a private in World War I, in the 163rd Infantry out of Montana in 1917, and assigned to the Observation Corps with the 103rd Yankee Division from Deven, Massachusetts. He spent two years on the front lines under General Pershing in five battle positions. He took Mustard Gas in the battle of Chateau Thierry on July 18, 1918, and unknowingly ate some gas tainted meat. He received care at the hospital in Mon, France, and was put back on the front with his unit in November of that year.

Little thought was given to the depth and range of the damage done to the fighting man's mental condition at that time. Mother Minnette, dad's new wife, was a nurse, but not trained in battle injuries. Her first interest was the welfare of this soldier's baby girl. She was in her forties and had given six years to a marriage of abuse and country living; the divorce was a glad relief. And when she set her plan in action, I was willing to go with her back to her family in Valparaiso, Indiana. That excursion was short lived before dad sent one of his family to bring me back to his old home town in South Dakota. But Mother Minnette never forgot me, nor did I let go of our connection.

The life and times of Private Driscoll went through two more marriages and divorces and four more children in the stream of Post Traumatic Stress experiences. He spent a lifetime of non-diagnosis for his condition in both mental and physical attention. The time came when the bossy little girl inside me would take it no longer. I found my way into the field of psychology and creative activity until a discovery of the sad story of mental illness came into the limelight — in particular with the military as more wars sent traumatic stress victims home from the battlefields.

True, this scenario had to be lived twice in my life, but the knowing and telling has a place in my *Chasing 'these' Shadows*. I want to give an insight to what I believe is a redeeming tool for the victims of this brain damage. I hope others can find their "Self" in the creative talents in each of us, and accepting the work it takes to value that damage. Medical and psychological fields are coming to the fore and we are not alone. Can we afford to neglect the hand writing on the wall?

— MDC

# In Appreciation

I am ever grateful to Alan Tucker for his portrayal in word pictures of this story inspired by my father, Private Arthur Francis Driscoll — WWI, 1917 to 1919. He, like so many veterans during that war and the following conflicts abroad, were praised as the returning heroes, only to be lost in oblivion with hurting memories — shadows of the hell they could not forget. Alan's word pictures create a "gallery show" of what took so many years to come into the awareness and treatment by the medical and psychological fields. Then, to do what was needed for the veterans who were inflicted with this haunting brain disease. It was first called "shell shock" in the early war, now to be recognized as "Post Traumatic Stress Disorder".

When more was known of the brain disorder by the psychiatric field, and accepted by the medical professions, there began a course of action to diagnose and help the Veterans. But there was still room for the soldier to grasp the nature of the condition and then, how was he to cope with this still disabling uncertainty. The memories brought pain and torment, hellish in themselves, but the uncontrolled behavior, which was not summoned, left scars on their outer life with family and friends.

How far afield this disease could go was a big factor society was unprepared to embrace. Getting a grasp on pain was one thing, and maybe the medication could make some difference, but the hellish shadows in the mind took more, and what that element turned out to be was different for each individual.

How can a person who has not been in the battle field give solace or compassion to a loved one who has gone through those experiences? It comes from the buddy of the battlefield, the accepting and merciful empathy of kindness. Some help has been found in the Service Dog giving unconditional love. Humankind has touch with this embrace, but more, much more, is needed to deal with that great pain. Just to think of the numbers of soldiers is a cause in itself. Recognition of damage to loved wives, children and others of close connections is still to be reckoned with. It was long years before I recognized the vicarious effect my father's war memories had on me and its effect on my life all of my ninety years. It is always with you. My painting, clay work, and writing have been mentors and solace to a grace given for living a procession of productive years.

It is with no hesitation that I give praise to Alan Tucker for his sensitive approach in shedding light on a cause so near and dear to me. As this condition with my father came to light in my sad awareness, I found a learning through the word, compassion.

— Marion Driscoll Cadwell